I0571776

ALONG THE FOOTWALL

Along the Footwall
Copyright © 2017 by Oak Hill Books

**Oak Hill
Books**

Oak Hill Books
PO Box 901
Raleigh, NC 27602

Oak Hill Books and its logos are trademarks of Oak Hill Books. All
other trademarks used herein are the properties of their respective
owners and are used for identification purposes only.

All rights reserved. No part of the material protected by this
copyright notice may be reproduced or utilized in any form by any
means, electronic or mechanical, including photocopying, record-
ing, or by any information storage and retrieval system without the
prior written permission of the copyright holder.

Author: Tilden M. Counts, Jr., Ph.D.
Foreword: Kirstin A. Counts, D.C.

Published by Oak Hill Books
Printed in the United States of America.
First Printing.

ISBN-10: 1-937258-12-2
ISBN-13: 978-1-937258-12-2

Footwall definition. American Heritage® Dictionary of the English
Language, Fifth Edition. Copyright © 2016 by Houghton Mifflin
Harcourt Publishing Company. Published by Houghton Mifflin
Harcourt Publishing Company.

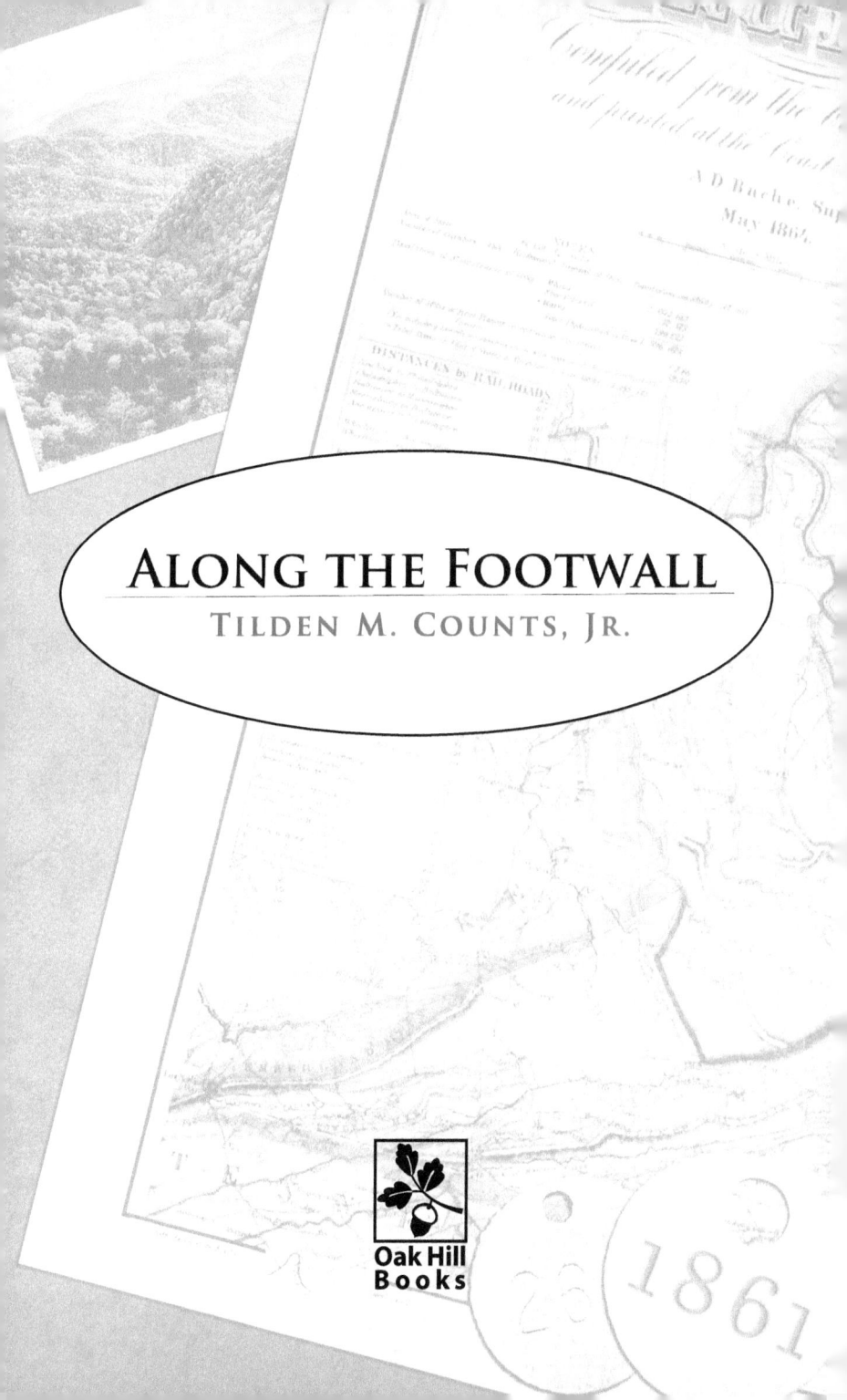

ALONG THE FOOTWALL

TILDEN M. COUNTS, JR.

Oak Hill Books

For Mona

TABLE OF CONTENTS

FOREWORD

When I think about writing a foreword for a book of my father's works, I find it difficult to know where to begin. If I asked Dad for advice, he would most certainly give me a familiar response from my childhood. "Well," he would say theatrically after clearing his throat, "begin at the beginning and stop when you come to the end." I usually found his paraphrase of Lewis Carroll's King of Hearts to be wildly entertaining, especially when it was directed at one of his students. Dad gave me lots of advice over the years, but that particular maxim left an indelible mark and has served me well on more than one important occasion.

No matter how helpful it was, this advice had a tendency to be rather nebulous. What Dad didn't tell me is that a lifetime is full of beginnings. Of course, there's birth. It's the big one that every human gets by default, but from a creative writing perspective, it's kind of low hanging fruit. The real meat of the story comes in with the many starts and stops and restarts that happen along the way. He gave me no direction about knowing which beginning is the right beginning to use. Regardless, his sage advice turned out to be most useful, leaving me plenty of room to tell any given story from a perspective that is distinctly my own.

So, I guess I will begin at the beginning…

My first clear memory of my father is of him at his desk, typing away on his old manual typewriter—the heavy keys with their long metal arms clunking and thwacking against the paper, punctuated by the loud clank-zip-ding of the manual return arm. Each finished page was sealed by the zip of the barrel as he pulled it out with a flourish and added it to the pile on the desk next to him.

To me, Dad's typewriter was a magical thing. I was certain that I would have arrived when I was finally allowed, or better yet, expected to create something on that typewriter. I would know that I finally was *somebody*. (Thank you, Steve Martin.)

In the dim glow of his desk lamp, Dad clicked and clacked for hours. His desk was perpetually covered with papers, pencils, pens, and his ever-present yellow legal pad. In my mind, Dad was always surrounded by stacks of books and papers. He had file folders filled with mysterious documents that I was certain contained vitally important and potentially classified information based on the fact that they were lofty enough to require their own folders. I am fairly certain there was a painted clay lump that my brother had made for him in art class there, too. It seemed that whenever he was in doubt about the true nature of one our childhood masterpieces, Dad used it as a paperweight. We were never disappointed. The top of his desk was prime real estate.

That image of Dad at his typewriter was a moment that repeated time and time again throughout most of my youth. I was never really aware of what he was writing. I just knew that he was writing and that the act of writing seemed to evoke as much anger and frustration as it did happiness.

It's important to note that writing was not his only passion. He explored many creative things over the years—photography, music, target practice—but like many of us who dare to endeavor in the arts, his creativity often had to take a backseat to his day job. He was good at his job, and it afforded him the chance to use his writing and research talents in his everyday life. I am sure that many people benefited from Dad's work as a professor, even if his job rarely resulted in accolades.

Over the years, Dad traded his manual typewriter for a word processor and then later for a computer, but the stacks of paper, books, and painted lumps of clay remained. Today, the prime real estate has been expanded to fit in the artistic masterpieces of his grandson and includes not only the top of his desk, but several bookshelves and walls, too.

Above all, Dad is and always has been a storyteller. Some of his best stories were the ones that were more like performance art than writing. I believe he never intended to write these stories down. They were told in moments of complete resonance with his audience and with his past. They were the product of profound introspection mixed with years of oratory practice which resulted in an experience of deeply emotional sincerity and nearly tangible imagery. Those stories, as they were when he told them, are lost to time, but I believe they affected everyone who heard them.

Over the years, Dad has written a lot, but the moments when he has been willing to unleash his works upon the world have been rare. Like many creative types, he was never fully satisfied with his creations which made pushing forward through the inevitable resistance that comes with self-promotion very difficult—if not impossible. It's not a flaw; it's just the way we are wired. I, however, am happy to push onward (with anybody else's work other than my own, most of the time), which is how this book came into being.

The stories in this book are what Dad called "shorts." They are fictional narratives based on historical truths and influenced by his own experiences. To me, they are like snapshots from our old Polaroid camera. They develop in your hands, right before your eyes. You know that eons came before them and that time will carry on after them. You can feel the impermanence of time's continuum.

For now, these are the only unpublished works of Dad's that I could find. Paper gets lost, and floppy discs are becoming harder and harder to access. I will continue the search, in my spare time, so that more of his creations can be brought out into the light. Until then, I hope that you will enjoy these moments with my Dad as much as I did.

Happy Birthday, Dad.

Kirstin A. Counts
March 2017

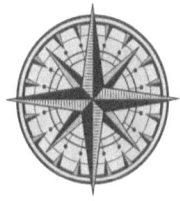

footwall *(foot'wôl') n. Geology* *1.* The mass of rock underlying a mineral deposit in a mine *2.* The underlying block of a fault having an inclined fault plane.

BORDER WARS

COLLEY AND OSBORN
SEPTEMBER 1780

"…if they did not desist from their opposition to the British arms, and take their protection under his standard, he would march his men over the mountains, hang their leaders, and lay their country waste with fire and sword."

Dispatch from Major Patrick Ferguson, Inspector of Militia in the Southern Provinces, British Army, 1780, to the Men of the Western Waters.

*C*olley heard a mockingbird call from a chestnut tree to his right as he made his way toward the edge of the woods. Past the tree line in a shallow brook, a woman was doing the wash. Suddenly startled, she looked up in Colley's direction. Colley cut his eyes toward the source of the sound and spotted a boy perched high on a limb in the shadows behind the coloring leaves.

The woman dropped the wash and shouted toward the three children who were playing upstream. She splashed through the water toward the them, snatching the smallest child from the ground and grabbing another by the hand as she hurried toward the cabin in the clearing.

Osborn was working in the garden behind the cabin when he heard his wife shout the alarm. He ran the short way to his long rifle that was leaning against the ancient oak tree that shaded the cabin. He seized the rifle and looked up to the tree line. Osborn held steady as he watched and listened.

As Colley emerged from behind the trees, he looked out over the homestead. The brook spilled down the hollow. In the distance, the spurs of mountain ridges beneath blankets of crimson, gold and yellow ascended under brilliant sunlight toward a distant father mountain. He dismounted and led his horse through the clearing and the short distance down the hillside to Osborn's cabin.

Recognizing Colley, Osborn set his rifle aside and called out to the cabin. The woman from the brook peered around the doorway and gazed up the mountainside toward their visitor. She stepped outside with the children following close behind.

The homestead was well established. A wood spit for cooking animals was off to the side near the cabin. A pot for stewing and cleaning sat on stones away from the spit and near the stream. Down by the stream articles of wear and bed clothing were draped to dry across tree limbs and bushes. Away from the cabin, at the edge of the woods, chickens pecked near a makeshift house that Osborn had fashioned for his animals. Two horses and two cows grazed on the hillside. The corner of the large garden stretched out from behind the cabin.

As Colley approached, Osborn waved him in.

"Welcome my friend. Come in for a bite of food," Osborn said, taking off his wide brim hat and rubbing a hand through his yellow hair. A short, pale beard shadowed his face. "We've got tomatoes and squash left over."

"Thank ye, Osborn, I'm fine," Colley replied. "I'm in a bit of a hurry."

"Well, you know Shessie and the children," Osborn said, opening a hand toward his family, who had stopped a short distance away from the men.

Colley touched his hat and tipped his head as he greeted her, "Miz Osborn."

Osborn's wife looked at Colley warily and then glanced back at Osborn to see if his face could tell her something more about Colley's unexpected arrival at their cabin.

Shessie was a sturdy looking woman. Her deep red hair was gathered and tied into a knot at the back of her head. Strands of white around her face foretold her own changing season. Beside her stood Osborn's oldest child, a freckled girl who looked to be about eleven years old and was likely the image of her mother in another, younger time. She had long, straight, auburn hair and was by any standard a pretty girl. Osborn's youngest, a little boy just beyond infancy, wiggled about in his sister's arms, his darting eyes seeking something he could treasure for a moment. Her younger sister held her hand and smiled up at Colley. Colley returned her smile.

The uneasiness that had been dogging Colley since he set out for Osborn's place began to stir. Shessie seemed to sense it and touched her children to move them back toward the creek and her washing.

"I'm here to speak with ye about a matter, Osborn," Colley said.

Osborn motioned and Colley led his horse to the shade of the massive oak tree standing near his cabin. The oak was tall with sturdy limbs. A rope had been doubled across a stout branch to make a swing for the children.

The two men sat on a log bench that stretched across

the stumps of two small trees Osborn had cut down. The smell of the nearby wood chip pile was sweet. Colley's horse wandered and grazed as the sun warmed the hillside under a clear blue sky. Osborn removed a pipe from his shirt pocket and began stuffing it with tobacco. He offered Colley a smoke, but Colley declined. Lighting his pipe and taking a draw, Osborn said, "Now, Colley, what is this matter you speak of?"

Colley thought that perhaps it was a mistake to come ahead of Bowen to warn Osborn, but he liked Osborn, liked his manner of speaking.

"Ye come from Scotland, do ye, Osborn?"

"When I was a boy," Osborn replied. "Ulster, most recent, though. No land for us. Couldn't get along with the Catholics, so we boarded a ship and came over. It was that or go back home to the Borders and renew the eternal fight with the English. No, Ulster's no place for a Scotsman, unless you're a rich one."

"My own granddaddy came from the Lowlands, like ye'self," Colley said. "Spoke with bitterness toward the English."

"Then your grandfather would recognize English justice in Tarleton's slaughter of Buford's company under the flag of surrender."

"He would've that, Osborn," Colley said. "But Buford's done with. Ain't nothing to be done about that now."

"Tarleton is the devil himself, Colley," Osborn went on. "That massacre showed him for his English way. He brooks no surrender." Then he added, in a moment of disbelief,

"The white flag, Colley. He killed those men as they begged to surrender."

Colley nodded. British presence and brutality seemed to be met with less defiance with each report trickling into the mountains from the south. South Carolina appeared to be turning against the rebellion and showing loyalty to King George and the Tories. Men and boys of the colony were joining Tarleton's and Ferguson's militias or were in others ways yielding to British protection...or they were fleeing, as Osborn had apparently done. Queer to think about such worries here in the mountains, Colley thought, where neither rebellion nor battle had visited.

"There's two devils terrorizing South Carolina, Colley," Osborn said. "It was Tarleton massacred Buford. But Ferguson's as bad. Mark my words. I want no part of either."

Osborn stood up, as if to pace for a moment, but sat back down and leaned forward looking toward his feet, his elbows on his knees.

Colley said carefully, "The situation down your way has gotten worse, Osborn. Gates has surrendered at Camden. Colonel Sumter a few days after that."

Osborn received the news of more Rebel losses with no emotion that Colley could detect.

"Then there's nobody left to fight," Osborn finally said. "South Carolina belongs to King George, now. All the rest of the colony will join a Tory militia or hang."

Colley said, "Ferguson's coming this way. He's made his move."

Osborn drew from his pipe, stared at the ground.

"Aye, he would," he said after a moment.

Colley added, "Says he's going to burn us out and hang us."

Osborn looked past his house to the stream at Shessie and the children. The two youngest children were splashing in the water and laughing.

"I need to warn ye. Bowen's on his way here," Colley said. "He ain't far behind."

Osborn looked at Colley. "Here?"

"The militia's been called."

"I'm not militia. I've not joined."

"Makes no difference."

Osborn drew on his smoke and looked toward his wife and children at the creek. Behind them across the hollow, ridges of color retreated to the distant horizon. "You know that for the truth?" he asked.

"Word is we're to go to Sycamore Shoals and meet with Shelby and Sevier. We're going to kill Ferguson," Colley replied.

Osborn took the pipe out of his mouth and appeared to consider. A bee buzzed near his head. Preoccupied, he swatted at it.

"There's no end to it I can see," he said. "It's time to leave, Colley."

"I came on ahead to warn ye," Colley insisted, "to give ye time to think about it."

"Nothing to think about. There's nothing in the way of the English between here and there."

"No, there ain't," Colley agreed.

"Ferguson will kill every one of you. It will be another slaughter," Osborn said. "If Ferguson is marching toward these mountains, what's to stop him? Save yourself, friend Colley."

Colley turned his eyes from Osborn and seemed to consider. "Bowen is goin' to make ye join with us, Osborn."

Osborn smoked his pipe as he contemplated the ground at his feet. At length, he shook his head. "I can't do that, Colley. I won't do that. I won't fight."

"He ain't a-goin' to give ye no choice. He's rounding up all the men he can get. He ain't going to ask."

"It won't make any difference, Colley. I'm done fighting," Osborn said defiantly.

"If the English come ye'll have to fight. Ye've got to fight, or the troubles will start up for ye again...like before," Colley replied.

"I understand what you mean, friend Colley, but I won't do such a thing. My aim is to find a place for my family where I don't have to fight. Where there is no fighting."

"There is no such place, Osborn."

Osborn raised his head and looked past the hillside into a receding valley visible from his place. His turned his gaze toward his cabin and the secluded ridges of the distant mountains.

"Like my father," Osborn said, "I won't fight. I'll take my family and move on."

It was plain to Colley that Osborn didn't understand what was to come. "Bowen ain't goin' to accept that," Colley insisted.

"Bowen will see it. I'd do him no good in a fight." A movement and a shout from up the hill brought Osborn to his feet. "It's my son," he said.

A boy ran out of the forest, leaping over stumps and across the paths that Osborn's cows had cut into the hillside. Colley recognized him as the boy who sounded the alarm from the chestnut tree. He looked to be about eight or nine years old. "Riders comin'," he said breathlessly as he approached the two men.

"How many, son?" Osborn asked.

"I don't know, daddy. Twenty, thirty maybe."

"It's Bowen," Colley said as he stood.

Osborn caught the look on Colley's face and turned to his son, who was looking intently at his father. "Go help your mother, son."

The boy hesitated.

"Go on, now."

The boy looked first at Colley and then turned to look toward the tree line. He looked back at his father for a moment before starting for the creek.

The two men waited in silence. Colley stood by his horse, patting it, unable to look at Osborn. The horse nuzzled him back contentedly. Osborn sat, smoking his pipe. A panther cried somewhere in the hills.

Bowen stepped out of the forest. He was a towering man who seemed even larger than the horse he led. A company of armed men appeared behind him leading their horses down the mountainside with an urgency in their pace. They carried muskets and long rifles with sacks for provisions slung across their shoulders and their horse's saddles. Osborn's cows moved awkwardly out of the way as they crossed the field. His horses were roped and secured after a short chase along the slope. Six men broke away from the band and followed Bowen down the hillside while the rest stayed near the trees.

Osborn stood and waved a hand of greeting. Colley turned to his horse and tightened the cinch. He checked the reins and bridle fitting, his back to Osborn.

As Bowen approached, he gripped the reins of his horse and looked at Colley. The horses began snorting and stamping the ground.

Bowen's reputation as a farmer with a growing herd of cattle in Fincastle was well known. As widely told was his reputation as a fighter killing roving bands of Shawnees threatening his farm and beating men to death with bare hands. Colley had wondered at the truth of the tales, but thought it wiser to assume them to be true.

Bowen turned to one of his men and said, "Watkins, take the horses down to the creek and tell the men on the hillside to take shifts at the water."

Watkins called out two of the men who took the reins

of the horses and followed him toward the stream where Shessie and the children were watching. The others wandered away to the shade of the great oak tree. They were bearded and dressed alike in dark colored spun-cotton pants and shirts that were open and rolled to the warm September day. Whatever else the men had with them they carried in bags draped across their horses. Colley had seen one of them, Samuel, before when he made rounds on his horse, bartering cut wood for food. Colley didn't know the rest, nor did he know most of the families in the mountains. The other men could have gathered coal for trade or worked a mountainside with a family, like Osborn, or they could have worked for Bowen. It was difficult to say.

"Osborn," Bowen said, "we need men with guns and horses. Get yours ready."

Osborn faced Bowen. "What is your hurry, Bowen? Why don't you sit a spell? Eat a bite with us. We have vegetables and biscuits left over."

"No time, Osborn. Ready your family for your absence. Go see to them."

"Can I ask, friend Bowen, what this is about?"

The men under the tree glanced at Osborn and Bowen. Colley waited for Bowen to act, but Bowen answered Osborn. "Ferguson's coming to burn us out and hang us."

"Then that's what he will do, friend Bowen," Osborn replied. "He will come and slaughter everyone."

"We're not waiting for him, Osborn."

Osborn looked from Bowen to the men beneath the oak

tree. They kept their watch about the mountain, but were clearly listening intently to Bowen's words. "Do you really believe, Bowen, that you can hunt down a British officer as you would a rabbit with men such as these and cause him any concern at all?"

"We're going to hunt him down and kill him, Osborn," Bowen said. "The militia is forming in Abingdon tomorrow and gathers with Sevier and Shelby in North Carolina in three days. Get your horse."

"Well," Osborn said, "I don't believe I can do that." Osborn looked toward Colley, as if expecting support, or at least, a comment.

Colley turned his eyes away from Osborn and saw Osborn's older son beyond the cabin, running up from the creek toward them, the young girl and the older girl carrying the baby close behind.

"You don't have a choice," Bowen said in a tone that struck Colley as curiously gentle. "We need you, Osborn. We need every man with a horse and a gun."

"My horse isn't fit for such use."

"We'll take you on foot. Half the militia don't have horses."

Colley understood that Bowen's momentary patience came from the need he spoke of. Ferguson would have to be stopped before he came into the mountains. Every man to fire a gun would matter. But Bowen was not a patient man.

The men by the tree stirred restlessly.

13

"I sense your alarm, Bowen," Osborn said, "and that of your men, but you are speaking of the English. There is no escaping them and their cruelty. I think we both understand this."

A movement took Bowen's attention. He saw Osborn's wife drawing close to the cabin where Osborn had left his musket leaning near the doorway, but she passed by the cabin quickly and approached Bowen slowly and warily. She stopped and stood behind Osborn with her children close behind her. The eldest girl held tightly to her brother, who pulled at his sister's hair. The older boy moved past them, as if to join his father's conversation, but his mother grabbed his shirt and pulled him back to her.

Bowen looked at Osborn's family. For a brief moment, Colley thought he saw a look of sorrow pass over Bowen face, but it was only for a second. Bowen then turned and went to his men standing by the oak's trunk. He spoke to them quietly. Colley could not hear him, but he sensed that the circumstance was about to change. One of the men began running across the sloping hillside toward the animal shed. Another started quickly toward the cabin. As Bowen watched them follow his orders, his massive frame slouched. He put his hands on hips as he straightened and then returned his attention to Osborn.

Shessie called out as the man entered the cabin. Her cry seemed to echo and then fade into the trees. Turning toward Bowen, her eyes wary, she said simply, "Leave us be." She pulled her children to her, holding to the older boy.

Colley saw the men at the creek look toward them, pull the horses away, and start up the hill. Osborn took the scene in and appeared to understand what he was seeing.

Calmly, Osborn said, "I hear that you have recently arrived, Mr. Bowen."

"I believe that you are the recent arrival, Osborn," Bowen said arrogantly.

"I mean to the colonies," Osborn clarified.

"A bit longer than yourself, I think."

"Then you know English nobility," Osborn said. "You knew lords and ladies?"

"Only those who owned the land I worked," Bowen replied.

"And they took from you and left you little for yourself."

"They did that, Osborn," Bowen said.

"And that is why you left, to come and begin a new life for yourself away from sovereign English, where you thought you could raise your family and grow your crops and herd without fear of plunder by your masters." Osborn continued.

Bowen looked steadily at Osborn. "That is exactly what I am going to do" he said coldly.

A sound broke from the cabin, and Bowen's man stepped outside leaving the heavy oak door standing open. He ran from the cabin and moved up the slope quickly toward the man now leaving the animal shed. Osborn watched without reaction, as if he refused to understand what was happening. Passing Bowen, they showed him their empty hands and shook their heads.

Shessie prodded her children closer to Osborn, as if to protect him, while holding to the boy's shirt with one hand and the younger girl's arm with the other. Her eldest daughter remained behind her with the baby in her arms.

Osborn turned to Bowen with his forgotten pipe still in hand. "You came to this country, descended from a ship in a harbor...Baltimore, I'll chance, and saw that the English were prospering in the city. They call themselves continentals, but even here, the English are masters of commerce and wealth. Bowen, hear me, it will never end. The English nobility have conquered the cities. They will conquer the land as they move westward. They will dominate, and you will serve."

Bowen's body seemed to thicken and animate, though he stood perfectly still. "I have my land, Osborn, as do you, and they will not take it. Fight with us. Save yourself and this mountain."

"Don't you see it is hopeless?" Osborn argued. "This land belongs to the English, and they will not rest until they have taken it back. They will, they have threatened, set fire to your homes, and they will kill you."

"What will you do, Osborn, when they come to burn you out and take your wife and children?" Bowen argued. "Will you fight when it is too late and there is nobody to help you?"

"I will take my family and move on," Osborn said, brightening, the look on his face suggesting he had misunderstood Bowen's intention.

"Where will you go? To the northwest and to the French?"

Bowen asked. "Or to the southwest and to the Spaniards. I'm sure they will both welcome you."

"There is open land," Osborn responded.

"From which you will have to move your family yet again. There will be no end to it, Osborn. Look at what you have," Bowen said. "This mountain is yours. Stand up for what you have now. Go with us. Help us find Ferguson. Help us kill him."

"I will take my chances and live with it," Osborn said, turning slightly away, as if he had closed a deal on a trade.

Bowen nodded to the remaining men at the base of the tree. One of them led a horse under the large branch that held the children's rope swing. The smallest man pushed off the horse's rump and leapt barefoot onto the its back and stood perfectly balanced while he took hold of the rough hemp rope. He pulled himself, hand-over-hand, to the tree limb that held it. He sat on the limb and began working the knot from the rope.

Bowen watched, then turned to Osborn. "Osborn, I believe you are a Tory in service to the Crown."

Startled, Colley glanced at Bowen, then to Osborn. Colley had not thought of that possibility—that Osborn was a Tory, or that he had come to spy for the Crown. He saw Osborn's face change. What the look meant, Colley couldn't say.

"What do you mean, friend Bowen?" Osborn asked incredulously.

"I mean, Osborn, that if I were a British general in

Caroline I would order families of the loyal militia to relocate northward into the mountains on the appearance of settling. I would order them to await my attack and then take up arms from within. That's what I would do, Osborn," Bowen said firmly.

Osborn glanced quickly toward his wife and back to Bowen, and then to Colley. Colley was turned toward his horse that was nodding and stamping as it sensed the tension in the hands that held him.

"Don't you see, Bowen?" Osborn said, laying out a hand, as if Bowen should take it. "The English would see no need to take such measures to defeat your militia. They think of you as barbarians. Ferguson has called you the dregs of mankind. Bowen, look at them. Your militia more resemble devils than men."

The man high on the tree limb stopped worrying with the knot in the rope that held the swing and pulled a knife from his pants. He cut the rope loose and let it fall beside the horse onto the dust. The horse whipped his head and turned it to the side as if to watch. The man on the ground picked up the rope and with swift, deliberate motions began wrapping the free end around the long loop that was hanging to the ground at his feet.

Bowen said to Colley, "Bring him."

"The cabin," Bowen called out, heading for the oak tree and pointing toward the men holding the horses. "Don't let them get the musket." One of the men ran toward the cabin as ordered but strained to look back toward the gathering under the tree.

"Get his horse," Bowen ordered, pointing toward the shed.

Osborn's eldest daughter began to cry. She placed her little brother on the ground and ran to her father. The older boy fought against his mother, whose strength and rising fear held him to her. The girl child clung to her mother, now crying like her sister.

"Stand up for me, friend Colley," Osborn pleaded.

Colley gently nudged Osborne toward the oak tree. Osborn moved back a step, bewildered, looking at Colley. His daughter clung to him as she cried. "Colley," he pleaded, "please don't."

Colley turned Osborn by the shoulders and shoved him toward the oak tree. The girl stumbled as she screamed and clutched at her father. Colley pulled him away. "No!" the girl wailed as hot tears streamed down her face.

Beside the oak, the man with the rope pulled the collar through its wrapping, opening the collar's loop. Someone threw the rope's end to the man in the tree, who cut off a length of rope and dropped it to the ground. He laid the rope in his hand quickly over the thick limb fastening it tightly.

Bowen's man at the shed appeared in the opening pulling a horse behind and holding what looked like a sack cloth in one hand. He walked the horse across the field toward the oak tree. Down by the creek, a breeze fanned a piece of clothing Osborn's wife had hung across a tree branch and lifted it, dropping it to the ground near the washing pot.

"Move your horse, Niall," Bowen ordered to a red-headed

man with a blushing face and freckles. Niall picked up the reins and led the horse away from the rope hanging from the limb. He tied the horse to a sapling close by.

"Tie off the others," Bowen said to him. "Don't want 'em spooked. You stand there and keep 'em calm."

Finished with his business on the limb, the man in the tree slid down the rope to the ground, gave the rope a tug, and seemed satisfied.

"Over here, Cullen," Bowen said, motioning to the man leading Osborn's horse. "Step it up."

Bowen took the horse, moved it around and positioned it in the track of the children's swing alongside the rope, holding onto the bridle with a firm grip. "Stand with Niall," Bowen said to Cullen. "Watch the horses, keep a lookout."

Niall leaned the muskets against the oak as Cullen pulled the horses to the saplings and tied them off.

"Bring him," Bowen said to Colley.

Osborn's wife gave out a cry as she began to waver. At that moment, the boy broke free of her grip and ran with his fists pounding into the nearest of Bowmen's men. Shessie pulled her daughters to her and silenced herself. Colley thought she might fall, but she stood upright, opened her eyes, and glared defiantly at Bowen.

"You murderer," she said. "You murderer," she repeated. "We've done nothing to you," she said, her voice rising but controlled.

Bowen steadied Osborn's horse. He looked at Osborn's wife and watched her pick the baby boy up from the ground. She embraced him as she held fast to her youngest daughter who was crying without understanding.

"Samuel, Hez," Bowen said to two of the men near him, "take Miz Osborn and the children to the cabin. Take them in and don't let them watch. Do you hear me, Hez?"

They nodded in response. Samuel picked up the boy who struck at him as he carried him toward the cabin. The man, Hez, who was nearly as big as Bowen, placed a heavy hand on Shessie's shoulder and took a step. She shook off his hand and said, "I'm not going. I'm staying here." She was quaking uncontrollably, her face white with fear. She glared at Bowen.

Hez bent and put an arm around her waist as if to lift her, but Bowen spoke. "Leave her be. Take the children." Hez tore the baby boy from her, bent again to pick up the eldest girl by the waist, and started for the cabin. The youngest girl followed, legs moving rapidly to keep up.

Bowen looked at Osborn's wife and appeared to consider something. He said flatly, "You chose to watch this."

She didn't respond, but glared at him as the muscles in her upper body trembled fitfully.

Bowen spoke to the little man who tied the rope knot onto the limb. "Flea, go take Cullen's place. Cullen," he said to the man watching the horse, "over here."

Osborn, seeming calm, said to Bowen, "Let us go, Bowen. We mean no one harm."

Bowen turned to Colley. "Colley, I said bring him here."

Colley took hold of an arm and placed his hand against Osborn's back. Pushing, he could feel Osborn's heat through his gray cotton shirt. He thought he could feel a pulse at the crook of Osborn's elbow.

"Cullen," Bowen said, "tie his hands and help Colley put him on the horse."

Cullen picked up the extra length of rope that was on the ground and began tying Osborn's hands. Osborn was turned so that he looked Colley in the face. Osborn's eyes were wide with growing terror, his skin white against his pale stubble of beard. Colley had to look away.

Positioned beside the horse, Cullen held Osborn under the armpit with one hand and held his leg at the knee with the other, and turned to Colley. "Hold him steady by the other arm while I lift." Colley grasped Osborn's arm and felt Osborn go light as Cullen lifted him suddenly onto the horse's back.

Bowen turned the horse and the two men so that they faced the cabin and Osborn's wife. The horse jerked uneasily, and Bowen steadied it.

Osborn's breath was coming in spasms. His eyes moved back and forth from Bowen to his wife.

"Please, Bowen, I'm not a spy," Osborn said, his voice breathless.

Osborn's wife dropped to her knees. She began to moan and to rock back and forth. Bowen pulled Osborn's head down to him and placed a sack cloth over it. He set the noose over Osborn's head, pulled the rope tight against his neck, and set him upright on his horse. Colley and Cullen backed away.

"I'll go with you, Bowen," Osborn cried out through the cloth, "I'll hunt Ferguson with you."

Bowen slapped the horse's rump. The horse jumped, bucking Osborn off its back before moving off to the side with the other horses. Colley heard a snap and Shessie's scream at the same time. Osborn's body twitched involuntarily as it swung to and fro from the limb of his oak tree.

Osborn's wife laid her forehead to the ground and sobbed.

Bowen watched Osborn hang for a minute, then turned to the men near him. "See to the horses and guns. Get ready." Bowen turned to Cullen, "Wait a while and cut him down. Bring him on your horse. We'll bury him a bit away."

He then turned to Colley. "You and Niall take Miz Osborn to the cabin. Easy with her."

She couldn't help them very much, though Colley noticed she was not as heavy as he thought she might be. They led her by the hewn log where Colley had sat only a few minutes ago with Osborn as he smoked his pipe and talked. Osborn's wife had stopped sobbing. She seemed to be in shock, but she was walking under her own power. As they approached the cabin, Colley could hear the children crying inside.

Bowen, on his horse, rode up along side the three of them. He said, "Gather your children, Miz Osborn. I'll have one of the men accompany you to Clive Holland's place where you and the children will be safe."

She shook herself free of Colley's and Cullen's grasp. "I'll go nowhere with anybody, Mr. Bowen. Leave us."

Bowen didn't speak, but waited.

"I said leave us, Mr. Bowen." She turned and stepped up into the cabin.

Bowen turned his horse and shouted, "Gather 'em up."

Colley's horse was grazing near the hewn bench. Colley noticed unburned tobacco on the bench where Osborn had tapped it out of his pipe.

Bowen moved up the mountainside and waited. Cullen made his way up the hill with Osborn's body tied behind him across his horse.

"Let's move!" Bowen commanded as he turned his horse and headed toward the tree line. His company of militia followed him into the forest.

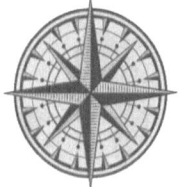

THE GIRL BY THE WELL

LESTER AND HEATHER

MAY 1861

*T*he road from New Garden meandered across gentle swells of rich, earthy farmland. The surrounding hillocks and sheltered vales of the valley were nestled between the steep, flinty mountains to the west and the low blue ridges to the east. New Garden was the county seat of government, and though it was small, it was growing and prosperous. Past the edge of town, there was a new saddler's shop with the shed of a successful blacksmith nearby. Beyond the shops and storefronts on a small bluff to the right stood a magnificent home. It was painted bright white, with a huge porch that wrapped three sides on the first and second levels, where the prominent Mr. Churchall and his family might oversee the town and admire the dazzling vistas. Across the fertile valley, the blue ridge rose before them. The road to Goodson was visible to the southwest, and they could watch the travelers as they made their way to the bustling railroad depot which was their lifeline to Richmond.

Just beyond the big white house, a trail forked to the right and plunged into a dense forest at the foot of the hollow. The fork was viewed by locals as the divide between the valley, snug against the graceful blue ridges on one side, and the steep and treacherous mountains of the Cumberland range toward the west. The trail was a narrow wagon path used by infrequent travelers from deep within the mountains. Shortly beyond the fork, it began rising upward in a series of twists and turns as it wound toward the top of the heavily forested mountain behind the town. Near the top, the woods opened at a turn in the trail. From here, there was an angled view back down into the hollow and over the valley.

Lester Merradew stopped the mule he was riding and dismounted. He looked down toward the town and found the grand white house with the wraparound porch and the beautiful green lawn of colorful flowers and apple, maple, and oak trees. The shadow cast by the late afternoon sun on the mountain left the hollow in darkness and extended the serrated edge of night close to the Churchall's back lawn. At the painted well with its brilliant white gilding was the trace of berry calico, where Heather had said she would be.

Ahead on horseback, Emory and Robert Merradew picked their way up the wide path that had been worn along the side of the ridge. It angled around the sharp sandstone rocks jutting out of the hillside and up into the pathway. The journey back home would move along more easily than their three-day passage to New Garden. Their mule had been slowed by their cart laden with goods for sale and trade: canned preserves and quilts and work shirts made by Mrs. Merradew; spring garden vegetables and bacon from their hogs; honey gathered from the bee combs in the mountains; and tools fashioned by Emory and his sons in his shed. Emory had sold everything, including the cart he had built to transport his goods, so the return would be quicker.

The forest near the mountain top was cool, though below, down in the little town, the day had felt quite warm. On the mountain, shadows and shafts of sunlight dappled the green of the fresh spring growth along the trail. Above the canopy of leaves, the bright sun shone and cotton white clouds hung lazily about the blue sky. The air was moist and rich with the aroma of warm loam. The woods were hushed with a tangible silence that emanated from the deep forest and traveled along the mountain slope.

The silence that had come between Emory and Robert on the way up the mountain was a welcome change from the heated conversations Lester had heard between them once he finally found them on the New Garden Road. His father had been restless and apprehensive. He was anxious to leave and furious with Lester for his tardiness. Brother Robert's face had been red with anger. Emory had withdrawn into a suppressed rage. Mounting the horses and aiming them toward the fork in the road, Emory and Robert had stayed well ahead of Lester and his mule as they argued, the undertones subdued, their words inaudible.

Lester looked hard through the opening between the trees toward Heather. She was there at the well, as she had said she would be. It was not that she could see him, but that she would be there for him to see her, until she was certain that enough time had passed for Lester and his father and brother to cross over the top of the mountain.

She was there. Her words had been true. Perhaps all of them.

Staring through the trees toward Heather, Lester caught a sudden movement to his side. He turned his head quickly and glanced behind him through the leaves of the overhanging limbs and across the path.

Two riders were approaching at a pace. One rider was uniformed in a red tunic with yellow trimming. He wore a cap of fur with a tail. Startled, Lester recognized Heather's father, Judge Churchall. The second rider was the deputy that had confronted Emory at the wagon as they were setting up for trade on the outskirts of New Garden. Seeing him, Lester realized in an instant why they were coming.

But there was Heather, down there by the well, the berry-color that she wore now riveting his attention, taking his breath as might the tiny jot of a jewel he could not name. He saw her by the white painted well among the splashes of red and white azaleas, blankets of bluebells, and the beds of early spring roses scattered about the bright green lawn. She was awash in sunlight, and she would remain there watching for him until she felt certain that he was beyond the hilltop and would no longer be able to see her.

"Riders, daddy," Lester said, the edge in his voice absorbed by the forest.

"Come along, boy," Emory responded quietly and kicked his mount forward. Robert, beside Emory, stopped and turned to look back. He stared toward the riders, his eyes and freckles the color of rust against his bright complexion and beneath his ginger hair. After a moment, he nudged his horse and reined up alongside his father.

Lester saw the fear erupt on his brother's face as the

two riders approached. The look that came over Emory's face sent a spear of heat that stabbed Lester's heart. An enormous dread appeared and spread within Lester, filling him like thick mud. He turned away from it and sought refuge in the reflection of white and the touch of berry calico that was Heather by the well in the Churchall's backyard.

It had been a day of revelry and jubilant celebration. Young men and boys with soft cheeks were yelping and yahooing as they fired pistol and rifle shot into the sky. They converged on New Garden on horseback, by wagon, and on foot to enlist and fight. Shooting contests flared on the main street and down side roads in festive celebration of "secession," which Lester didn't understand, and the new "confederacy," which he understood only to be new and important. The thump of cannon fire reverberated inside Lester's chest as it hurled an explosion onto the hillside across the creek behind the town.

The town itself was exploding with skyward gunfire and smoke and shrieks of delight. Fiddlers played along the wooden walkways by the storefronts. Adults danced in the street, releasing shrieks of excitement. Pretty girls under parasols gathered near a large gray tent where a line of young men and boys had formed. The boys entered the tent, one after another, and exited out an open flap in the back, appearing no different save the expression of uncertainty on their face. Colorful balloons blew about and barefooted children raced among the revelers as if this day would be the standard against which all those to come would be measured.

Riding into New Garden, Emory Merradew led the mule pulling the cart into an opening by the side of the road among other wagons and carts driven in by farmers and tradesmen who were busy setting up their wares. Buyers were moving up and down the road, examining goods at the wagons that were already set up.

In front of the Merradew cart, a sunburned, fair-haired man with a pale beard unloaded sacks of salt-cured pork from a small wagon. A boy not much older than Robert was staking a stretched canvas tarpaulin to the ground between the wagon and the road. A younger boy, freckled, slight and barely older than Lester, led a team of horses into an open hayfield behind the wagons along the side of the road.

"My boys are enlistin'," the fair-haired man called out to Emory, "just as soon as we git ourselves set up here. They're a-goin' right down to that courthouse and signin' up." He looked up at Robert on the cart. "Ye got some fine lookin' boys ye'self."

Emory glanced at the man and lowered the side of the cart facing the road without speaking. Lester was staring toward the uproar in the center of town at the courthouse, where crowds of people were gathered in the road in front of the shops and stores. He could hear gunfire and see a large gray tent stretched across the middle of the street between the courthouse and the frontage of general stores and shops.

Impetuous Robert, with a look of glee on his freckled face, leaped onto the cart and looked toward the courthouse, shading his eyes from the glare of the sun off the dusty road. "What is it?" he asked excitedly.

"It's enlistment day," the fair-haired man said. "I brought my boys for enlistin'."

"For what?" Robert asked. He seemed energized, despite the three-day trek over the mountains. His normally pink and ruddy skin was flushed red with excitement, drawing out the freckles, an appearance of goodwill that fooled the unwary.

"Why, South Ca'lina has took Fort Sumter," the man said, as if Robert should already know that. "The Union has give it up. We're at war."

"Robert," Emory said sharply, though quietly, "tend to the cart."

Robert didn't respond. Raising his voice, Emory said, "You hear me, Robert?"

"Yes, sir," Robert answered, his face flaring to a brighter red.

"Go find water for the horses and that mule," Emory said, "then you come back here and help me get set up. Lester," he added, lowering his voice, "go find some crates somewhere."

For Lester, the spirit of celebration did little to add to his keen anticipation at seeing Heather again. His previous journey to New Garden had been in the brilliant colors of autumn, before the winter snows and rain rendered the transportation of goods to New Garden nearly impossible. Heather had told him then that she would wait for him in the spring on every trading day that farmers came to town to market their goods. She would wait for him on a bench against the azaleas under a tree on the courthouse lawn. As a parting gift, she had given him a pad of sketching paper and a packet of drawing pencils and charcoal. Lester had had no gift for her but she didn't seem to mind.

Lester was in front of the wagon folding the shirts his mother had woven for display and Robert was off the tarpaulin laying out honey combs on boxes that Lester had found, as a burly man approached them. Emory was behind the wagon hanging up the horses' tack.

"What's your age, boy?" the man asked. He had sun-leathered skin and brown eyes under thick brows. His stare was invasive. He was tall and wore a straw hat pushed back on his head. A bulky pistol was holstered at his side, and a star badge showed at his chest.

"Sir?" Lester said, turning around.

"Your age, boy. How old are ye'?" The look on his face indicated to Lester that his age was the man's business.

"Fifteen, sir, and I'll be sixteen next month."

"Ye' look a damn sight tall for fifteen, though a bit delicate for fightin'. Don't matter, ye daddy can sign for ye."

Robert's back was to them. He broke into the exchange as he said loud enough for the man to hear, "Why it's ye lovely green eyes he's makin' reference to, Lester."

"For what, sir?" Lester asked quickly, more to intercept Robert, who could hurt the man, as to find out what he was talking about.

Just then Emory came around the tailgate of the wagon. Emory was tall, and his wiry frame gave an exaggerated range to his movements that were both spare and, at the same time, graceful.

Emory looked from Robert to Lester to the man, and asked, "You want somethin'?"

"I want your boys, mister, especially the bold one with the sassy mouth. They need to be in that tent up there where ye see all the commotion," he said, tilting his head toward the bustling town, "and signed up."

Robert took a step toward the man before Emory stopped him by quietly speaking his name.

Turning to the man, he said, "Well, they ain't goin'. Now, is there anything else here you see you might want?"

The man, taking offense, looked back at Emory. "Ye older boy, there," the man said, nodding toward Robert, "I want him to follow me up to the tent."

"You pressin' him into service?" Emory asked quietly.

"Won't be long," the man said, his leathery face warming to red.

"Then move on," Emory said, "unless there's somethin' you see here you want to buy or trade." Emory's face had flushed to a bright red and the knuckles of his hand holding a hammer had turned white.

"Keep ye tongue, mister," the man said. "Judge Churchall deputized me to see that Colonel Falkerton's 37th Virginia gets filled to the quota with boys to fight, and that's what I'm doin'."

Emory shook his head and said, "They ain't goin' with ye, deputy. Now, that's final." To mark his words, he turned away and laid the hammer into the wagon's bed.

Walking away, the deputy said, "I'll be lookin' for that big boy at the tent. And I'm a-goin' to check on the age of ye other young 'un."

Emory turned to Robert and Lester, looking hard at each one of them from silver blue eyes set in his angular face. "You stay away, you hear?"

"But, daddy," Lester said. He was at once fearful that he wouldn't see Heather.

Emory turned sharply. "What?"

"I got to give Heather the pictures I did for her." He had made sketches for her with the gift she had given him. "I promised her, daddy."

"Aw, let 'im go, daddy," Robert said, chiming in, "he's too chicken to fight and his little girl'll see to it he don't get into no trouble."

Lester almost laughed. He could have hugged his brother and taken the slug he would have gotten for it.

Emory looked at his young son and took him by the shoulders with both hands. "They can't take ye, Lester," he said. "You ain't old enough. You understand me?"

"Yessir," Lester said, his heart suddenly racing. He was going to get to see Heather, after all, and he struck out past the wagons along the road and into the town.

The courthouse was a two-story, pine wood and brick building set back on a level above a grassy embankment in the center of town along the main road. The courthouse lawn was taken up by farm and town boys in rags or fine clothes, as their personal circumstances allowed, whiling time away in groups talking, playing mumblety-peg, or shooting marbles on a sandy spot they found. Lester walked among the groups looking for her on a bench, where she had said she would be waiting for him. As he wandered around looking for her, more boys came onto the lawn and joined those already there. They were coming from the back of the large, gray canvas tent set up down the embankment as the people swarmed swarmed main street in celebration.

"Just waitin' for orders," said a fair-complexioned, barefooted boy with long black hair and blue eyes, stretched out under the shade of an oak tree. He was sitting alone and whittling shavings from a piece of cherry wood. Lester thought the boy couldn't have been much older than himself.

"To do what?" Lester asked.

"Shoot Yankees, I reckon," the boy answered, drawing laughter from a group of older boys on the grass nearby.

He walked down the wooden steps in front of the courthouse onto the plank walkway along the street and felt a tap on his shoulder. He turned and looked into the face of a woman who resembled Heather. Suddenly embarrassed and feeling awkward as a child might before an adult, he saw that it was truly Heather, her blue eyes clear and pale like the sky, her face now somehow different, with new and startling angles.

She looked up into his eyes for a moment, saying nothing herself, her eyes wide, now darting this way and that across his face, her own face, for an instant wavering as if in wonder, suddenly bursting into a smile to match the celebration going on about them. Then she said, "Lester, you are so pretty."

He didn't know what to say, his mouth unable to form a word were his thoughts able to find one. They stood there, bumped and elbowed by the milling crowd, seeming not to care. Then Heather took him by the hand and said, "Let's go."

She led him through the celebration out onto the main road where men in linen coats and straw hats and women in finery were stirring and chattering among farmers and mountaineers in rough clothing. Lester did not think there could be so many such people in New Garden. Most of the men and boys were dressed in everyday work wear, but some of the men were frocked in long-tail coats, top hats and string ties, and many of the ladies appeared to be in fine style beneath their bonnets and umbrellas. He noticed that Heather's dress was the style that an older woman might wear, though a soft, pale blue with tiny white checks. Her black curls, loose and free of a bonnet, bounced at her shoulders as she paced ahead of him, pulling him along, holding his hand through the crowd, carrying a bag in her other hand.

They were passing through a line of boys by the big gray tent when a sharply uniformed man suddenly appeared in front of Heather, stopping her, the momentum carrying Lester into her. The man wore a sheathed sword at his side and creased black pants. His black boots had obviously been polished to a shine beneath the dust that was gathering there. His light blue tunic was pressed and sharp and had red stars sewn onto the stiff collar. He had a handsome face and held himself with an air of authority. He appeared to Lester to be a few years older than Robert.

"And where are you off to, Miss Heather?" he asked, smiling at her.

Heather returned his look without a smile and without speaking. As she started around him, he grabbed Lester by the arm and said, "The enlistment tent is right here, at your service, young man."

Heather gave the man a piercing look and said sharply, "Press, turn him loose."

The man she called Press held onto Lester long enough to make a point before letting go of his arm.

She led Lester across the street to another wooden walkway, now along the fronts of the merchants' stores away from the center of town, where the large groups of people were fewer. She turned swiftly between two stores and followed a darkened alleyway that led them down a grassy bank to a stand of willow trees shading a flowing creek behind the buildings. She let go of Lester's hand, bent over and removed her shiny black shoes, revealing her feet, bare of stockings, jolting Lester's heart. She grasped the bag she was holding and led him through the woods along a path beside the rocky creek running behind the town.

He followed close behind her, watching her, thinking of a doe as she bounded nimbly over the path and around the undergrowth. Moving swiftly, she held her skirt hem up to her knees revealing cotton pantaloons she wore underneath.

He wondered at her tiny waist and the way her skirt curved around her hips.

She stopped in a shaded dell where the creek ran slow and where a pool had formed at the base of a gentle limestone water fall. Shafts of sunlight dropped through the willow trees that hung over the creek and the light gleaming onto the water. They stood on a grassy flat near the stream. The air was still. Its shaded silence was adorned with trickling eddies bubbling around the stones scattered about the creek. The cannon fire and rifle shots seemed distant.

Heather dropped the bag she was carrying and turned to Lester, breathing swiftly from the run along the creek. She gripped her fisted hand with the other and pressed both hard to her lips, her hands trembling. She looked into Lester's eyes, her eyes gleaming. Lester stood looking at her, unable to speak, not knowing what to say to this girl before him, this woman, who was his age, but not his age.

"Lester," she said, "I am so sure." Her face softened, and she dropped her hands away from her face and clasped them to her chest. "You are so pretty," she said again.

He said, voice shaking, "I thought about you all winter." It was all he could think to say, speaking for the first time since she found him at the courthouse. He hadn't thought before he spoke and was sure he sounded foolish. He felt even more inadequate before her and had an impulse to run.

"I am so sure, Lester," she said. "I want you to meet my father."

She handed him the bag she was carrying and said, "I brought you some clean clothes and soap. There's some cloth to dry with and a brush."

She took his hands in hers and brought them to her chin. "I'll go into the woods and wait," she said, and turned and ran into the shadows.

He realized his own clothes were dirty. Looking at his hands, he saw they were covered with the grime of work. He had not bathed since before he and his father and Robert had left their mountain home three days earlier. They had worked the horses and the cart of goods over the mountains and slept on the rough trail to New Garden. He was embarrassed to know that Heather had seen him that way. Self-conscious, looking about him to be sure he was alone, he removed his pants and shirt and the leather shoes his mother had fashioned. He jumped into the creek and felt the brace of cold water stir around him. He sat and felt his muscles go weak and drifted in the pool before ducking under.

On the flat, he pulled out the trousers and shirt Heather had brought him and was embarrassed again, for he had never worn clothes woven by someone other than his mother or sold in a general store.

"Let me see," she said, as she came out of the underbrush. Looking at him, she smiled.

"I brought you something, too," he said. He picked up the three rolls of sketch paper he had placed beside the old clothes he had cast off, and hesitating with uncertainty, he handed them to her.

She took the rolls and unfolded them on the grass, first one and then the other, studying each one carefully. He had drawn with the pencils she had given him and etched with charcoal the likeness of the face of a fox. It was the first sketch she had opened and she stared at it, barely breathing. She stared at the second sketch with the same study and intensity. It was of a waterfall over a rock ridge as viewed from below. But it was the third sketch of her face in fine detail that brought her to look at him in wonder.

"Oh, Lester," she said. It was all she said.

She rolled them up carefully and then said, "I have something to show you." They walked side by side out of the dell, glancing at each other, until the path to town by the creek narrowed.

The path followed the contours of the shallow creek. Water flowed swiftly around boulders and over flat rocks in the creek bed, trickling and bubbling on its way. A huge rainbow trout hovering beneath the surface of the water by the creek's edge caught Lester's eye. The air beneath the trees was cool. Shadows and sunlight speckled the pathway.

Lester thought that he would like to take Heather to his home in the mountains and show her the waterfall he had drawn. It fell a hundred feet from an overhanging precipice near the top of the mountain to a basin of rocks below. There, the water pooled before continuing over the hillside into the swift running creek that flowed beside his parents' cabin in the narrow valley in the hollow.

Heather moved them quickly along the path. The town was above them on a ridge to their right. They could hear the celebration ongoing along the main street. The cannon thumped and they heard the distant roar of the spectators' approval. There was a rush of air overhead followed by an explosion that boomed on the hillside to their left. Lester recoiled. Heather only flinched.

As they rounded a laurel bush, they came upon three men standing beside the creek. They were holding knives, and Lester thought they might have been whittling. Two more men beyond them squatted next to the creek in the shade of a willow. Rifles leaned in disarray against a log beside the path. The man closest to them saw them first. He was a large man wearing a gray button-up jacket and a worn felt hat with a turkey feather stuck in the band. He had three green stripes sewn onto the sleeves of his shirt. He wore a round cap with a black bill. The other four men had on similar shirts of varying colors. They all wore dark trousers and work boots.

Lester, already roused by the cannon's sudden discharge, heard Heather breathe in sharply, and his heart skipped. Her grip tightened in his hand. Lester wished to himself that he had not left his musket back at the wagon. It would have been foolish to bring it along with him to see Heather, and it would have been useless against these men, but he wished it nonetheless.

"We got visitors, boys," the large man with the turkey feather said quietly. His tone was menacing.

As if alerted to trouble, the other four turned toward them. The two men under the willows walked toward them and stood on the path blocking it.

"Hello, pretty miss," a young man said, and turned with a snicker to the others, shedding his boyish sneer when the others didn't laugh.

Now terrified, Lester could feel his heart racing, and though he felt bound to swallow, his throat tightened and he couldn't.

Heather stepped in front of Lester, holding onto his hand behind her. He felt her hand trembling in his. Her shoulders were quivering. He could smell her hair, like a gardenia flower.

"Lordy, look at her," one of them said, taking a step toward her. They all looked toward Heather as if Lester wasn't there.

She asked, trembling, "What are you doing here?"

Hearing her voice shudder as she spoke, one of the men giggled and the others seemed to rise up, roused. The large man with the turkey feather stared at her.

"She's a fine looker, sergeant," said a tall man standing by the path. He had a blond fuzz growing on his face.

Heather spoke again, but in a way Lester had not heard before and did not expect. "I asked you what you are doing here," she said again, her hand still trembling in Lester's.

Lester could see they were going to hurt her and stepped up beside her, gripping her hand tighter, looking for a stick, a rock, anything.

"My father owns this property, from there," she said pointing up the rise toward the buildings along main street, "to that hill over there," pointing in the direction of the blue ridge. Her voice was strong, but Lester felt her wobble against him as she looked to the left toward the ridge.

The men chuckled at her dismissively.

"Judge Churchall," she said firmly.

They broke their stare and glanced at each other. Lester heard one of the men say, "the captain."

"Captain Churchall?" asked the one called sergeant.

"Yes," Heather said.

The sergeant turned to her and said, "Miss, our orders are to keep people away from this part of the woods under that cannon fire. It ain't safe. It would be better if you and your friend moved on to safer terrain 'til it's over."

The two men blocking the path stepped aside. Heather pulled Lester past them and down the path.

They ran along the creek that flowed behind the main street until Heather suddenly started up the hillside toward the road. Trees thinned, and they were past the buildings and the line of wagons and tables where the farmers and craftsmen were dealing their wares along New Garden Road. Lester was aware that Emory and Robert were there among them, but Lester did not want to see them, lest his father take him away from Heather and put him to work. A smoky pall had formed above the revelers inside the town.

Heather led him past the saddle maker's shop that smelled of turpentine and across New Garden Road. She continued up the roadway toward a huge white house at the top of the bluff. Out of breath, she slowed the pace, and they walked remainder of the carriage way to the house.

"This is where I live," Heather said.

The house was huge, looming three stories high with

four chimneys rising toward the sky. The whiteness of the mansion's paint and its metal roof reflected brightly the midday sun like a snow bank on a dazzling winter day. It hurt Lester's eyes to look at it.

The grounds surrounding the home were like nothing he had ever seen. The grass was lush green and cut low. A white picket fence lined the perimeter. Colorful flowers surrounded the mansion's foundation, and beds of color lay here and there on the green lawn. The lawn behind the home extended to a border of grape arbors that marked the bottom of gentle hill. Beyond the crest of the hill loomed a steep and craggy mountain to the west, the mountain Lester called home. Tiny white clouds hung above as if suspended from the pale blue sky. Lester had never seen such a vision. He realized that his own cabin, where he lived with his parents and his brother Robert, was the size of only one of the rooms of the mansion where Heather Churchall lived.

A colored man was working a hoe in the grape arbor. Two other negroes were on their knees digging into a spring garden that extended from the corner of the ground. Green sprouts of beans, lettuce, carrots, and corn were showing above the rows. The smell of turned earth and cut grass was in the air. A spring house sat near the garden in the shade of several tall maple trees.

"I'm thirsty," Heather said. She took Lester's hand and walked beside him along the graveled carriage way to the rear of the mansion. A negro woman stood at the doorway, as if she had been waiting for them to appear. A long carriage barn was set beyond the mansion under several sprawling oak trees.

"Kizzy," Heather called out, almost playfully, "we need water, or we'll die."

"I knew it," the negro called Kizzy replied, "and I brought it right out when I saw you two strugglin' up that carriage drive." She held out a silver tray holding two glasses of water. The glasses were wet with condensation, and Lester was compelled to keep his hands to his side, lest he appear wrong somehow. Kizzy was young and the color of his father's coffee with a dollop of cream in it.

Kizzy glanced at Lester with what he thought was a look of disapproval. He thought about what he might have done wrong and could not think of what it might be. Heather gave the girl Kizzy instructions regarding dinner, to prepare something that might be suitable for warming since her father might be late coming home that evening. Heather's tone issuing the instruction was one of genuine authority that intimidated Lester. He did not know if he was up to this woman, for that is what he had come to think of her. He wondered what Kizzy thought.

Kizzy said, "Yes, m'am," when she received her instructions, but added, glancing toward Lester but not looking directly at him, "Ma'rse John not gonna like it." She quickly lowered her head and looked down at the tray of empty glasses she held at her waist.

Lester was startled by the girl's comment, and part of him felt like bolting. Heather, one fist at her hip and the other arm at her side, looked at the girl with affection. She said gently, "I know, Kizzy, but I can handle father."

Kizzy kept her head lowered. "Yes, m'am," she said.

Sending Kizzy back inside, Heather turned Lester toward the back lawn and the stone well painted white with red trimming.

"I told you I want to show you something," Heather said, taking his hand again and walking along beside him, "and then I want to show you off to daddy."

A gate in the fence beyond the grape arbor opened onto a gradual rise toward a nearby tree line on the hill above the house. Limestone boulders jutted here and there out of the cleared ground and then stopped at a cluster of small boulders. Heather turned to take in the view across the valley, and clasped her hands in front of her.

"Isn't it so beautiful?" she said.

Lester had seen narrow valleys before where steep mountains came together. He had seen craggy cliffs and long shadows cast against their rocky faces by the sharp afternoon sun. He had looked over the edges of cliffs into narrow hollows and into rocky gorges cut deep into the earth by flowing waters. But Lester had never experienced the gentle softness, the roundedness within the valley, flowing like a placid stream beside the serene blue ridge.

"That belongs to us, Lester," she said. "All of that. To the top of the blue ridge yonder." The high point was a rock formation extending out of the end of a break in the ridge, looking like a train's engine pulling a long chain of dark blue freight cars. "We have cows in the valley and fields of wheat you can see." She pointed southward across the valley where he saw a large grain field emerging. "We have negroes to work it all."

Rifle fire sounded far away, and smoke was visible below and to the left over the town. The cannon gave a distant, muted thump.

She was looking over her mansion, across the valley toward the blue ridge.

"How do you do that, Heather?" He had sat down on a rounded boulder that suited him.

She turned her head to look down at him, her pale blue eyes soft, her cheeks round and moist and pink from exertion, the lines along her blue dress round against the sky.

"Make it belong to you?" he said.

She gave a look of puzzlement and said, "We just do. We've always had it." She shrugged, "Grandfather gave it to us."

Lester looked again at the valley and the ridge and wondered at what she said.

She sat down on a small boulder across from him and looked directly into his eyes. "I mean it belongs to us, Lester. You and me. It will."

He thought a moment about what he heard her say, arriving at a meaning. "I don't know how that can be, Heather," he said because he decided he didn't know what she was talking about. But taking in the valley and the sky with Heather close to him holding both his hands, something else was awakening in him that he also didn't understand.

"All of this is too much for daddy by himself," she added.

Lester was aware that Heather's mother had died years

before, and her father was alone with Heather to raise.

"I manage the house servants and the grounds" she told him. "I pay the bills and keep the farm accounts balanced, just as mother would have, if daddy had wanted her to and she had lived. I buy what we need. Momma wouldn't have done that, but I do. So, daddy doesn't have to worry about it...and now the war..." she said, and looked down. She looked up at him, again, with determination on her face. "I'll have to take care of all of it, and I will. The fields, too."

Lester thought that he himself could take care of his own family's farm on the hillside if his daddy and Robert went to war and that he would know what to do, even if his mother were not there. He could keep the hillside cleared, firewood chopped, the cows milked, the horses fed and sheltered, the pigs from straying, the garden plowed and hoed, the bees tended, the cabin weather safe... But Lester could not conceive of what Heather would be facing inside her mansion, or even more, from the mansion to the far ridge.

He saw the woman before him and thought that she could surely do what she said she was going to do. Her face flushed pink beyond exertion, it seemed to him, and she appeared nervous.

"I want you with me," she said suddenly. Her face blushed red and she looked at him as if entreating him to help her.

He questioned in his mind what he might be able do to help her on her farm, or plantation, or whatever it should be called, but he knew he would help her in any way that he could. His father and Robert could work the family farm without him for a while.

"I will help you," he said.

"I want you to marry me, Lester," she said. She pulled his hands to her mouth and looked at him as if she meant to burn his face with the force of her stare.

He looked at her, struck dumb, staggered by her boldness and the words he was trying to comprehend.

"Daddy wants me to go to a finishing school in Richmond, but I don't want to leave this valley. He said if I won't go to school, he wants me to marry Press Crager when I turn sixteen, but I don't like him. I can't stand him. We rode to the point on the ridge last Sunday, and he tried to kiss me, but I slapped his face."

Lester rose up, disoriented by an image of someone trying to kiss Heather, confused by the bewildering revelation that it mattered and by the rage and the trace of fear that passed through him. He tried to think what he was. Was he a boy as he had thought? Or was he a man, as Heather seemed to think?

He looked down at her standing before him facing him, close to him, gripping his hands closely to her mouth, all his thoughts afire on his face. He couldn't speak.

Heather searched his face for her answer and found it. "Let's go see daddy," she said.

Entering the grape arbor, she told a negro holding a pair of cutting shears to have Sam prepare a carriage and to wait at the kitchen door.

Lester waited in the kitchen extension at the back of the mansion, where Kizzy had met them before, while Heather went inside the house. Heather had said he could refresh himself if he wanted and told Kizzy to make available to him whatever he required while she went upstairs to freshen herself.

Kizzy placed a pan of water and soap and a fresh-smelling towel on a sideboard next to a large tub, which he used to wash his hands and face. The clothes that Heather had brought to him still looked new and fresh.

"You own slaves?" Kizzy asked him

"No, m'am," he said and blushed, not knowing exactly how he was supposed to address her.

Kizzy looked at him for a moment, a hand on her hip. She said, "You goin' to take care of her?"

His heart pounded. His face felt hot with the revelation that something new and utterly unanticipated was happening to him.

Shortly, Heather entered the kitchen, and for an instant, he was unable to swallow or to draw a breath. She had freshened herself, reshaped her hair, and changed her clothes. She had on a calico dress the color of nearly ripened blackberries. He could almost taste them. He saw a pretty little train of calico trailing her as she turned to Kizzy to remind her about dinner preparations. Her white blouse looked like it was lace over cotton, and it buttoned to her neck. He felt embarrassed and clumsy before such refinement.

"Isn't he beautiful, Kizzy?" she said, walking easily toward him. Her loose blouse hugged her forearms, and she had a white purse in one hand. It looked like silk. In the other hand, she was holding the drawings he had brought to her.

"Yes, m'am," Kizzy answered.

They rode in the back seat of the carriage down the curved drive to New Garden Road and turned toward the town. Heather sat beside him, her hands holding the purse and his drawings in her lap, looking every bit a lady. Lester sat thinking of his appearance, aware that at any minute the carriage would pass the Merradew cart. Heather might recognize his father and his brother selling their farm goods by the side of the road. But more than that, he did not want his father to see him.

Heather leaned forward and said, "Sam, take the road behind the courthouse," as if she knew what he was thinking.

Sam turned the bay left and drove the carriage down a short road lined with rose bushes and magnolia trees before turning right onto the street that ran behind the courthouse. The gun shots had diminished. Lester could see main street between the stores and shops. There were fewer people on the street, and the line of boys at the enlistment tent was short.

The courthouse was a large, new, two-level, brick structure. The back lawn of the courthouse was covered with camellia and rhododendron shrubs and beds of red, lavender, and white azaleas. Sunlight streamed through the sugar maple and pin oak trees dappling the scene with shade. Horses and carriages occupied a special place behind the lawn, where negroes stood in groups, some dressed in colorful formal clothing. A shaded wood plank walk led to brick steps and a landing to the heavy oak back door.

Lester followed Heather inside and down a long hallway

with polished oak floors. They passed the closed doors to the front entrance where a bright staircase with polished cherry wood banisters turned back and upward toward the second floor. As he turned to follow Heather up the staircase, Lester looked out the window by the front door and down onto the main street, bright with colorful parasols of ladies strolling in the sun. The top of the enlistment tent over the bank of the courthouse lawn fluttered gently in a passing breeze. Before turning away, he caught a glimpse of his brother Robert sitting on the lawn among a group of boys beside a bank of azaleas blooming red.

At the top of the stairs and directly in front of him was a closed door with the word "courtroom" stenciled onto its translucent window. A hollow quietness filled the empty building, unsettling Lester over and above the disquieting sense of power and privileged authority that permeated the courthouse.

Past the courtroom, the landing turned right, taking them down a hallway past closed office doors, whitewashed plaster walls, and red cherry banister railings. The last door was beside a hall window overlooking main street. On the door were the words "John W. Churchall, Circuit Judge." Lester's heart pounded in his head, sounding to him like the rush of swift water down a rocky creek.

Before opening the door, Heather looked up at him and smiled, as if to reassure him. Following her, Lester stepped inside the doorway.

Lester's eyes went directly to the man standing behind a large desk, small stacks of paper placed carefully before him. The man was of moderate size, as tall as Lester, and sturdily built. He was clean shaven but for a small, graying mustache on an evenly shaped face and blue eyes the color of Heather's eyes. Though the impression he lent was youthful, his long hair was gray and brushed over strands of black. He wore a red tunic that appeared to serve as a uniform, unbuttoned at the neck. Stripes were sewn onto the shoulder of his jacket, but Lester didn't know what they signified. On the wall behind him was a portrait of a man, an arm extended, standing in a black coat beside a table holding a quill in an inkwell, a red cloth draped over the side exposing a corner and a leg. Lester recognized the high forehead and firm expression of President Washington, from another time. Lester let his shoulders relax, and he took a deep breath.

"Heather Catherine," the man said with a smile, extending his arms toward her. His voice was smooth and clear, and to Lester, gentle.

Lester watched Heather move quickly around the desk to the man, and they hugged. He kissed her on the forehead and smiled.

"I knew you'd come," she said as she looked up at him, her own eyes alight.

"My sweet Heather Catherine. How could I not? The war be hanged, for my little girl. The enlistments can proceed quite well without one Captain Churchall, I'd say." He held her at arm's length and said, "Now, what is the occasion you have called this meeting for?"

Though Lester thought the question was asked with genuine affection, he was nevertheless embarrassed that he was the center of an occasion before Heather's father.

Stepping back and turning to Lester, Heather said, "Father, this is my friend, Edward Lester Merradew."

The eyes that looked at Lester for the first time were indeed gentle and the face pleasant. Churchall said, "Welcome, Edward Merradew, to our little town."

Lester nodded his head and said, "Thank you, sir."

"Tell me, Edward," the judge continued, "where you are from? I don't believe I am familiar with the name Merradew, except," he said, looking down to a stack of papers on his desk, "for a Robert Merradew, who has joined our cause by enlisting in the 37th Virginia this afternoon."

Startled, Lester let a moment pass while he tried to understand Judge Churchall's words. Lester's face turned bright red and without thinking, he said, "No, sir, daddy wouldn't let him."

For an instant, he thought his legs would fold beneath him as he realized he had contradicted Heather's father and argued with a judge all in one careless moment. Not willing to look at Heather for judgment of his behavior, he kept still and looked at the judge, as his father would have wanted him to do toward any man he might face in a difficult situation. However, there was nothing he could do about the heat on his face.

"That's all right, Edward," Churchall said, "your brother is of age and is a fine looking young man. He will do well, and I am sure the war will end soon. By fall, I've heard said."

"Father has been appointed a Captain in the 37th,"

Heather said entering the moment, "and will look after him. Won't you, father?"

Churchall looked at his daughter and said quietly, 'Of course, Heather Catherine." He turned to Lester. "Colonel Falkerton will lead the 37th. The colonel is a prominent landowner and a fine gentleman. He will be a first-rate officer," he said and added, "I am sure he will look after all of his men."

"Father," Heather said, "look what Lester did." She moved aside the stacks of papers on her father's desk and began unrolling Lester's sketches, one on top of the other. "Aren't they beautiful?"

Though he had looked as if he was about to say something else to Lester, Judge Churchall turned to Heather and stepped to her side, looking down at the sketch Heather had spread atop the others. Judge Churchall looked and tilted his head one way, and then the other. He leaned closer to the sketch that Heather called the still life, showing in lines and shaded detail the fox's face.

The judge bent slightly, as if for a closer look, and stilled Heather's hand as she started to move the sketch aside to display another. He looked closely at Lester's sketch before indicating with a movement of a hand that he would like to see the others.

He looked at all of the sketches in the same way, without speaking, looking at each picture closely, paying particular attention to the portrayal of Heather. Finally, he stood upright and looked at Lester. "Have you had art instruction, Lester?"

"No, sir," Lester answered.

"You made these sketches having no instruction?"

"Yes, sir," Lester answered, unable to decide if he had made a fool of himself for letting anyone see his drawings. Lester was aware that Heather was smiling, and took comfort.

"Yes, father, he did them," Heather said, her face beaming.

Judge Churchall looked at his daughter for a moment and looked again to the sketches. His smile was gone, as he appeared to be pondering something. The judge's brow wrinkled and he looked again at his daughter.

"I see," Churchall said.

"Do you like them, father?" Heather asked. She was looking up into his face.

He turned to her, his face soft, and said gently, "Of course I do, Heather Catherine."

She hugged her father and walked slowly around the desk. Stopping at some distance between her father and Lester, she had formed a triangle among the three of them. Turning to the judge, she said, "Father, Lester is from the Eagle's Nest region of Cain Mountain. He tells me it's beyond Copper Ridge, near Kentuck. His father is Emory Merradew and his mother is Alafair."

Churchall looked at his daughter as if reflecting on what she had said.

"Thank you, Heather Catherine," he said. He evened the corners of the stacks of papers on his desk before speaking and finally looked at Lester.

"I am pleased to meet the dear friend of Heather Catherine, and I thank you for taking the time to visit with us and allowing us the privilege of seeing your sketches. You have a remarkable natural talent, Mr. Merradew. Perhaps before long, when our responsibilities to this war are done with, we can sit down and talk, and I can learn more about you."

"Thank you, sir," Lester said.

With that, Heather gathered up the sketches from the desk and went to her father and hugged him, her back to Lester. Lester thought she whispered something to the judge, but he couldn't be sure, and saw only an affectionate smile on the judge's face.

They left Heather's father in his office and exited the courthouse the same way they had entered. Heather's steps beside Lester were deliberate, as though she were deep in thought. But then her gait quickened, and she seemed herself, in the way that Lester was more familiar. She smiled and placed a hand at his elbow.

Outside, the shade beneath the oaks was longer as the early afternoon had worn on. They were nearing the carriage when Heather said, "I believe it will be all right, Lester."

At that moment, he decided that he would try to become what this woman thought he was.

"How soon can you come back?" she asked.

He said, "I'll need to help daddy this summer, and we'll need to get ready for the winter. Is that what you mean, Heather?"

She held his sketches out to him, but he told her to keep them. "I did them for you."

"I'll try to have everything planned," she said. "When you top the mountain, look for me at the well."

He helped her aboard the carriage, and Sam snapped his whip above the horse. As the carriage began to move, she turned toward him and said, "Hurry back, Lester, and we'll go berry picking."

Lester watched her until Sam turned the carriage toward the main street taking her out of sight. He walked around the side of the courthouse and saw that the front lawn was crowded with the young boys and men who had joined up to fight. He walked around the grounds several times looking for Robert but did not see him. He thought that perhaps Heather's father was mistaken, that Robert had not enlisted that afternoon after all.

As the two riders approached the Merradews on the trail near the top of the mountain, he heard his father say in a low voice, "Come here, Lester."

He had begun to pull the mule to the side of the trail when the deputy called out, "You, Robert Merradew..." His voice was jarring, roughened, as a man with fear might bellow toward a foe. "You are under arrest."

Lester had taken the mule off the trail to the slope against the hillside. As the two men moved past, he looked up to see Judge Churchall's face and his easy smile looking down at him.

"Hold, Sparks," the Judge said and held up his hand.

To Lester's horror, he saw his father with his musket barrel leveled in their direction.

"Lester," Emory said again gently, "come here."

Lester obeyed and walked past the bay holding the deputy, looking up at him as he passed. The deputy's face was hard, and his eyes were wide. They darted between Robert and Emory, paying no attention to Lester as he led the mule by.

Lester heard Judge Churchall's voice. "Mr. Merradew, my name is John Churchall. I'm a district judge, appointed to serve as captain with the 37th Virginia Infantry. Your son enlisted in the 37th this afternoon by signing his name to an enlistment form drafted by the governor and forwarded to this county for execution. Doing so, Robert has offered himself for service in defense of the state. Please ask him to step forward and come with us."

Emory didn't respond and a silence followed. Lester concentrated on the occasional clink of the fasteners on the horses and the muted tap of hooves as the horses shifted their balance.

Lester took his place beside Robert and turned. The look on the deputy's face had taken on a wild force that unsettled Lester even more. He cast his eyes to the side and could still see Heather by the well on Churchall's back lawn. He wanted with all his might to turn his mule toward the mountains, go home with his father and brother, and return to Heather as soon as possible.

"Mr. Merradew," the Judge said, "I will accompany Robert to the 37th with no charges to be filed against him. This incident will be forgotten if he will return with me now."

There was a long silence before Emory spoke. "It ain't our fight, Judge."

At Emory's words the deputy spoke out, "Robert Merradew, I'm placing you under arrest for desertion. Step forward, sir."

The deputy's horse moved forward toward Robert. A shot exploded at Lester's right, the detonation stabbing his ear. Smoke erupted from the cap at the hammer of Emory's musket and out the barrel. The blast shook Lester, and its piercing report echoed throughout the mountain, scattering birds to flight and leading them away into the valley, ricocheting repeatedly before dying in a distant place, far away from the girl at the well.

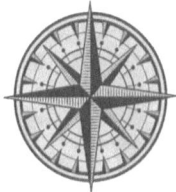

LILY

1921

A soft breeze drifted through the open doorway, softly ruffling Lily's thin white dress with pale blue daisies. She rocked gently, watching the baby feed and gazing at it in wonder as it suckled. She teased the corner of its tiny mouth and took pleasure from its random fits of movement and the fresh smell of the bath she had given it.

She had begun to nod when she heard Earl's footsteps on the planks of the porch. Startled, the baby drew away with a fuss. Lily glanced toward the doorway to see Earl move rapidly past Tolley playing on the porch and step quickly inside.

He moved quickly past Lily and the baby, not looking at them, something on his mind. Ignoring Garly at the table eating a jelly biscuit, Earl passed through the kitchen doorway to the wall behind the coal stove, dropped to his knees, and moved aside the washboard and tub he kept against the corner.

"Earl," Lily called softly. She could see him from where she sat rocking the baby, through the doorway to the kitchen, down on his knees, his back to her. She set the baby to her again, and the whimpering stopped.

"Earl?" Lily said again, a little louder now.

"What," he answered, not asking. He reached behind a hole in the wall and pulled out a crowbar.

"Earl, look at me."

Earl turned his head toward her. Lamp black and coal dust ringed his eyelids and smeared his face. Behind the grime, he looked afraid.

"Why ain't you at the mine?" she asked, the way she might ask Garly why he didn't clean the dirt off his feet when he came inside from drawing water or playing in the creek.

"Ain't nobody there," he said, poking the end of the bar to a crack in the floor.

"The tipple's soundin'. The train's a-takin' coal," she answered.

Across the road, a train lurched and coal cars clattered against their couplers up and down the track as they had in monotonous intervals through the afternoon.

"I can't help that."

Earl set the crowbar to the edge of a plank in the floor and pushed down. The plank broke loose with a screech from the nail holding it, and Earl pulled it free.

"You said you wasn't goin' to get involved."

"I know I said it. Don't mean I can't change my mind."

"You said you wasn't goin' to get involved," she said again. She sat up and brushed a strand of blonde hair away from her face and settled the baby closer to her breast.

Earl reached into the dark beneath the floor and pulled a metal box from the small space between the floor and the ground. He opened the box and tossed it aside with a clatter against the boards of the kitchen wall.

When he drew back there was a pistol in his hand. Lily saw the pistol and watched him tentatively clutch the handle. He gripped the revolving chamber and pulled the gun close to his eyes, as if to see better something he seemed uncertain about.

Lily stood up from the rocker and went over to Earl, holding the baby close to her. The thought came to her that her milk could be spoiling from the sudden spurt of something sour inside her when she heard Earl come upon the porch. The burn inside her felt the same as the gush of acid that had turned her stomach the night the man came to their house and talked about unionizing. When he had left, she was filled with a dread.

He had talked about unions and about how John El would lead the miners against the mine owners and John El wouldn't go timidly into the fight. He talked about fair wages in real dollars, instead of camp scrip, and fair costs for goods at the company store, and fair weighing the coal. But he didn't mention the massacre in Matewan, or the killing when the miners tried to organize there, or the company's hired goons wearing company badges and carrying guns and eviction papers. He didn't say anything about the wives and children put out into the street with all their belongings.

Lily had listened that night with growing fear. She watched the windows, expecting the company's police to knock on her door. Soon, tired and frightened by the talk, she had left

71

Earl and the man and lay down on the bed with her baby and little Tolly. Garly, who had been listening from behind the bedroom door, climbed onto the bed with her. They could hear the talk through the thin wall to the next room. She covered her children with her under the blanket Earl's mother had quilted for her and pulled them to her.

In the corner of the kitchen, Earl stood up without replacing the board he had taken up from the floor. The pistol was still in his hand. He went to the window opening by the sink and pulled aside the plastic covering.

"Earl," Lily said again, raising her voice. The baby stopped suckling. "We talked about this. You said the man was crazy if he thought you was goin' to get killed for a union." She looked at the gun in his hand, saw his hand shaking. "It ain't our fight, honey."

"It is, Lily. It's been talked over. The man has sent off to Cincinnati to get us a charter. We decided. We got to stick together on this."

Lily felt her arms weakening and cradled the baby closer to her. "The men ain't decided anything, Earl," she said, tears forming. "You all squatted in a circle and passed the liquor around till somebody said let's go get our guns."

Earl turned and seemed to hesitate, then said, "I got to go, honey." He looked at her and she thought she saw that he didn't want to go. He turned and looked at Garly, still at the table. Garly, mouth open, biscuit crumbs catching on his mouth, watched his father. "See to Tolly," Earl finally said, glancing toward the open doorway. Tolly had stopped playing and was watching them from the porch.

Earl sat on the window ledge and dropped to the ground. He looked back at her, then turned and ran. Lily saw his long brown hair and slender back move away from her. She watched him go quickly through the little garden of beans and tomatoes she had planted.

Quickly past the garden Earl began to climb up the steeply rising hillside, sweat pasting his work shirt to his flesh. His coal-gray form seemed to merge with the earth. Above and ahead of him was the tree line below a ridge. Overhead, small tufts of gray clouds moving across the sky signaled a rise in humidity.

"Momma, where daddy go?" Garly asked, holding pieces of his biscuit in both hands.

"I don't know, baby," Lily answered.

She watched Earl turn toward the trees above the entrance to the mine at the end of the row of board homes. Her parents lived in the last house of the row of company houses extending down toward the mine entrance. Earl seemed to move slowly, his form so near and visible, that her back tensed. She herself awaited the bullet that could so easily find him against the hillside, still below the trees and within sight of the offices of the mine superintendent and the company police.

She saw to Garly, gave him a fresh cup of water, and carried the baby to the bedroom, thinking that it was best not to dwell on the matter, but she was unable to think of anything else. She laid the baby on the bed she and Earl shared and began to fold the patchwork quilt, admiring the brightly colored squares of material and the skill of her mother-in-law.

She heard Tolley call her name from the front, and then she heard the footsteps on the porch. She stood upright and turned toward the sound. She saw a tall man standing in the doorway. She looked for Tolley but couldn't see beyond the form of the man blocking the light from outside and her view to Tolley on the porch. He was wearing a gray coat that hung open to his hips and a black vest with a badge pinned above the heart. He had on a shirt and tie. A dusty hat remained on his head.

The man moved his coat to the side, and she saw a pistol tucked into a holster strapped to his leg. He stepped into the front room, stopping beside her rocker, and stood looking into the bedroom at her. Behind him, four more men wearing badges stepped inside her house, the smell of oil and leather invading the room with them. They were not as carefully dressed as the tall man, but they were all carrying pistols in their hands.

She picked up her baby, the men circling her, seeming to imprison her, giving her a sensation of suffocating. She could not yet see Tolley, but she could see Garly at the table in the kitchen, his fingers squeezing biscuit pieces that crumbled into his lap. He sat still, watching one, then another, as they moved through the house.

Realizing she had not covered herself after feeding the baby, she pulled her open dress over her breast, her face hot with embarrassment. The tall man stepped into the kitchen and went to the window where Earl had left. He tore aside the window plastic from the nails above the opening and looked out.

Lily moved quickly around the men, avoiding touching them herself, afraid of being touched by them. She took Garly by the hand and pulled him away from the table and pulled him between the men who had entered her house, who now took up most of the space inside the kitchen and front room. They looked at her blankly, waiting to be told what to do with her, and let her pass onto the porch to Tolly. Outside on the narrow plank porch, several men with pistols strapped into holsters by their sides stood about. A small group of men milled about the yard looking up and down the road, each one with a shotgun or rifle in hand, as if expecting something.

Her flowers were destroyed. They had kicked through the marigolds she had planted within a ring of river stones next to the road, uprooting them, the bed of bright yellow and golden blooms strewn about. Earl's wood fence was pushed over for no reason that she could see. He had put it up one Sunday afternoon and painted it white.

Terrified, she stooped and lifted Tolly, holding him and the baby in each arm. Garly, standing behind her, his biscuit lost and forgotten, clutched at her dress and pressed his face into her thigh. Across the road, the train cars of coal clattered and screeched, rocking their way slowly out of the camp, load after load, going about business, the raid on her home disregarded.

A calloused hand gripped her arm holding Tolly and pulled her forward toward the door, pushing her into the house once again. Garly, holding on to his mother's dress, stumbled along behind. She turned back to help him, but the grip on her arm forced her toward the window Earl had climbed through a couple of minutes earlier.

She stood before the man quaking, unable to control the trembling through her body. Her breathing came in uneven gasps she couldn't control.

He dropped the plastic window covering and turned to her, reaching inside his jacket pocket. "This here warrant directs me," he said, "to remove you and your belongings from the premises." He pushed a sheet of paper toward her. She saw writing in curls that she couldn't read. There was a signature at the bottom she couldn't read.

"I am further directed to tell you that your husband has been discharged from the mine. You are to vacate the premises immediately."

She was so close to the tall man that she could see shaving scrapes and a rash of burns under his chin and along his neck. He had a rank smell about him like old sweat. A noise turned her attention, and she saw her rocking chair being lifted and carried toward the door. The pillow that she sat on while she rocked the baby slid off the chair to the floor. The pink blanket her mother had made for her when the baby was born was on the floor and under the boots of the men passing in and out of the house. In the sleeping corner of the room the mattress and springs were lifted off the board slats and carried out the door. The slats crashed to the floor, carelessly dropped from the side railing Earl had fashioned for their bed.

"Stop it," she screamed. The baby began to cry.

The dinner table where Garly had been eating was turned over and carried toward the door, the biscuits and jam scattering along the floor. Her iron skillet and pots and pans were tossed into the washtub and onto a blanket and carried outside. The picture of Jesus and the Disciples from church she had framed and hung on the wall was pulled down and thrown out a window. She watched a man pull out the drawers from the chest Earl had fashioned for her and take them outside, clothes falling out and left where they fell.

At the coal stove in the middle of the kitchen, two men carelessly shoveled ashes, scattering them, a gray dust rising into the room. The stove pipe leading through the roof was taken off the stove and tossed aside. With the sound of splintering wood from the corner behind her, she understood. They were looking for a weapon. To find it, they were taking up the floor beneath her.

She stood terrified, unable to move, until the man took her elbow and moved her away. Then, one board after another was pulled up until the earth beneath the board planking was fully exposed, hard and cold. Everything was gone.

Tolly hid his face in the flesh of his mother's neck, a hand on a breast where he had known contentment. The baby lay silent in her arms. Garly wrapped his arms around her and clung to her. Her legs weakened, and she thought that she could not hold herself upright. The feel of her babies against her seized her and paralyzed her. She stood in helpless terror and rage, clutching her children.

The thought occurred to her to run, cry out to Garly to hold on with all the might in his little fingers, and flee, Tolly and the baby safe in her arms. But the thought had come to her many times before, as she sat on the porch with her babies around her, waiting for Earl to come home from the mine. Most days he came in after dark, sometimes after midnight. A few cents pay for a ton of coal loaded was not enough money to quit work before shift's end. Every day his body ached, so tired he did not feel like washing himself. Some nights, when the morning shift was to start up in a few hours, he lay down without cleaning, falling asleep, to rise before dawn to go to work with the other miners in a procession, their column of head lamps flickering and weaving in the dark, lighting the path to the entrance to the mine.

Evenings she would wait for Earl and look across the dusty road and across the rail tracks to the creek that flowed down the hollow. She thought in her fantasies that they could follow the creek down to the basin in the valley. Or Earl could build a boat and the five of them could sail down the creek to find a better place, maybe a place where Earl could farm, like his daddy used to do. They had some land once.

Those were her thoughts one afternoon. The babies were quiet and the air was still and her reflections seemed real. Suddenly the parked rail cars across the road lurched, shrieking, startling her, and they began to move. She could not stop looking at the rail where she had imagined her family crossing to make their escape to the creek. She realized in that instant that she would be holding the baby and Tolly while crawling beneath the rail car. Garly would be crawling by himself under the car. He would have to cross the rails quickly, obeying her instantly. Caught under the car, she would not know what to do if the train suddenly heaved, screeching above her, not an arm's length away.

"Where's your husband?" said the man, folding the warrant and shoving it back into his pocket.

Lily answered, her voice quavering, "Earl can't do nothin to you," Lily said. "He can't hurt nobody."

A thickset man with a blond beard and a holstered pistol high on his hip stepped in front of her and interrupted.

"We ain't findin it, Pross," he said. "They was a board took out behind the stove and a metal box layin' on it, but if he kept a gun there, hit's gone now." The man in charge nodded, and the thick man walked away.

"Go on outside," he ordered her.

When Lily didn't move, he pointed to one of the men near the door. "Take her outside," he said. His hand waved Lily away.

"This is my home," she said.

"Not no more it ain't," he said. "You was told not to get mixed up with this union business. You was told what would happen if you listened to union talk. Now, go on outside."

"We can't hurt you," she cried. "We're just miners."

The man turned away and went outside.

Hate raged through her with a current that made her dizzy. She clung to her babies, felt Garly holding on to her.

A deputy standing nearby took Lily by an elbow and pulled her toward the door. Garly fell onto the overturned coal stove and scrambled up crying. Blood was on his mouth. He ran to his mother as she was led down the steps and into the yard.

Up the road toward the mine entrance a chattering sound erupted, followed by individual pops and yells. Lily recognized the sounds as gunfire.

Shouts broke out from the men around her. "You people was warned," one of them yelped.

A man standing near Lily looked over her head and said, "You want us up there, Pross?"

"Stay put," he said and looked at Lily. She took a step backward. "Listen to me, now. You give me the name of the man that came into your house and talked union to ye."

"There wasn't no man," she said. She lied. Her Jesus heard her lie. She was ashamed of lying, for the lie was not going to change anything. Her home was in rubble, her possessions scattered in the road. If the lie could do any good at all, it would be for Earl. Where was Earl? Panic gripped her, and her pulse throbbed in her throat. When he left through the window, she hoped that he might go on across the mountain—to some place and for some reason he had not mentioned. But she feared that he had taken the hillside above the mine entrance where the guns were now firing. She thought of her father and wondered if he was with Earl.

"I know that to be a lie," the man called Pross said. "We had him followed around. Red-headed man, said he was from Cincinnati. Went into your house last week, sometime around midnight."

Lily didn't speak.

"You're clear about what's happenin' here?" he said, his face close, looking directly at her. "You been evicted. You don't have no home no more. And if your husband's up there"—he pointed toward the mine entrance—"he's likely gettin' hisself killed."

The man drew himself up and started to walk away. "It don't make no difference to me." He turned back to her. "You go on, now, and git off the mine property. All of it. If they's any of this stuff here you want," he waved a hand toward her possessions strewn in the road, "you take it with you now cause you can't come back and get it."

The baby and Tolly felt heavy in her arms, so that she thought she couldn't hold them much longer. Garly, still clinging to her dress, stopped crying and watched the men. Around her she heard the sharp clicks of bolts chambering rounds and hammers being set.

More chattering, stuttering pops sounded up the road, beyond her father's house, near the mine entrance.

"Where am I to go?" she asked, but the man had moved away from her, on to other business. The men began following him along the road toward the gunfire, their own guns at ready.

She watched them leave, numb, with no idea what her next move would be.

"Ma'am." One of the company's deputies had stopped beside her. She looked up at him. He was armed and wore a badge, like the others. He spoke softly.

"There's a tent city over the mountain yonder and down a ways into the valley." He said the word there hard and flat, like she was used to hearing, like he was from her home place back in the mountains. He pointed behind her, down the road, the way out of the camp. "There's folks like you. Ain't nothin' but a dirt floor. It'll keep the weather off ye."

"My daddy is here," she said blankly.

"No, ma'am," he said quietly. "Nobody can stay that's been evicted. They'd just hurt ye some more and evict ye daddy too, if they ain't already." He looked at her a moment and said, "I'm sorry, ma'am. I been where you are." He turned and walked away, following the others ahead of him toward the mine entrance. The chattering of fire ahead of them had become sporadic.

She looked at her possessions in the road and then to her house. The house looked dark and empty. Boards that had covered the floor inside were scattered about the yard. She went into the road and looked for something she might keep. She had photographs of Earl and the babies somewhere, but she didn't know where to look for them in the pile. She knew she didn't have the force in her to look.

Their clothes were scattered everywhere in the road. She set Tolley down and picked through her belongings until she found one set of shirts, a pair of socks, and a pair of pants for the two boys. She found two cloth diapers near a large sack in which she had bagged a few potatoes earlier and set aside. She put everything into the sack of potatoes and held out the sack to Garly, who took it in one hand, trying to hold on to Lily's dress with the other. He would have to drag it, but she didn't have the strength to tell him.

The rage she had felt began to drain from her. She looked toward the house that had been her home, where she was rocking the baby minutes ago. It looked like a shack, now, her possessions scattered in the yard looking like trash.

Where was Earl? she wondered. Above her the clouds had thickened, showing a gray underside. Still, the sun shone through, its heat boiling waves off the dusty road and burning her arms and neck. She searched for the pink blanket, finding it under the leg of a bedside table in the yard, and covered the baby with it. She found a shirt and put it on Tolley, whose skin felt hot to her touch. She helped him put it on.

She stood in the road and looked up the hill where Earl had gone, but she didn't see him. Down at the mine entrance the gunfire had stopped and the mine was silent. She felt she should go to the mine and find Earl, or her father. *But what would she do with her babies?* she wondered.

Without realizing it or thinking about it, she had begun walking down the road toward the rising hill out of the camp. The rise looked far away, and her steps seemed to make no difference. The sun bore down on her; the baby whimpered and fussed. Tolley was heavy, and she set him down on the road. Garly followed along holding the fuzzy lamb he slept with that he had found in the rubble.

It seemed to Lily that she had been walking toward the rise a long time, though when she stopped to rest and looked back she saw that the camp was not far away at all. Her belongings were still in the road. They had not been picked over yet. She could see her house, the company store, and the tipple beyond the far end of the camp. Clouds began to cover the sun, and dark clouds were building high over the mountain.

She moved on, though the baby was feeling heavy in her arms. Tolly had walked a while, stopping to look at things, his short steps slowing her, and she had to carry him to get on. He felt hot. Garly followed behind as she walked. She had no food for them but the potatoes Garly carried. She wasn't hungry anyway.

She had gotten them on their way up the mountain when she saw Earl ahead of her. He was squatting, waiting for them beside the road. Garly, seeing his father, called out and ran ahead of her, hugging his father's legs.

"They evicted us, Earl," she said, coming up to him. She was glad to see him, but she felt tired.

"I seen it," he said, not looking her in the eye, his hand on Garly's head.

"Do you know about daddy?" she asked.

He shook his head, still not looking at her, and took Tolly and the baby from her. The weight off her arms, she felt as if they were lifting higher before they dropped wearily to her side.

"Was there a fight, Earl?"

"You need to rest, Lily?" he asked, not answering her question.

The forest stood thick with tall trees and underbrush to each side of the road. She thought she could make a place for herself to rest, but the road was dusty and would shortly be mud from the rain now gathering in the building clouds. She shook her head and took hold of Garly's hand. "We need to find someplace to stay, Earl."

The climb was rising steeply, and the road began to switch back on itself as they ascended the mountain. They had lost sight of the camp behind a ridge somewhere down the mountain. Thunder rolled close by.

"I seen what happened, Lily," Earl said, his eyes toward the road, not looking at her yet. Lily held on to the baby. Earl was holding Tolly. Garly gripped Earl's trouser leg as they walked.

She suspected he must have been in the trees on the hill above the camp when the shooting started and was not in the fight. She did not believe he saw the men come into their home and wreck it. Still, she thought, he might have seen them.

"There wasn't nothin' I could do about it," he said.

Clouds overhead darkened and seemed closer upon them. Lightning that had been flashing in the distance now struck close and the day around them darkened, the shadows in the woods deepening.

Looking for protection, they left the road and went into the forest. Shortly, above the road, they came upon an outcropping. Earl left Lily and the children under a shelf of sandstone and returned shortly with branches he had broken from trees. He leaned them against the outcropping and went for more limbs and branches, fashioning a crude shelter when he returned. When he had finished making them a place they lay down under its cover and sensed the heavy darkness coming. Drops of rain began to fall, gentle at first.

The wind quickened and soughed overhead, gusting

through the forest and whipping the trees. Darkness surrounded them so that they could not see. Lily felt rainwater rolling in tiny streamlets down the sandstone rock that supported their refuge, and into their nest through the covering branches and limbs. Earl had still not looked at her before the darkness set in. For the first time since she had walked away from her possessions, she thought of them lying in the road.

She lay over her baby and Tolly, supporting herself with her elbow, and felt Garly beside Earl.

Her baby suckled beneath her. Tolly began to cry. He was hot with fever.

"Shh, baby, shh," she said to him, and stroked his brow.

ASA
1929

*A*sa sensed the presence of the mule before he detected the shadowy outline of its head at an opening off the main shaft.

"Uncle Morgan," he called out and waited, listening, hearing his echo return from its search of the mine that had been drifted into the mountain.

Uncertain, hesitating before the blackness, Asa's eyelids flared open. Asa stepped forward into the opening, trailing his hand along the side of the mule and then along the wood slats and iron fasteners of the cart behind the mule. Blind in the darkness, he didn't see the sloping ceiling and bumped his head, sending the hard hat Uncle Morgan had given him clattering off. He stumbled over shifting rubble and fell, sharp edges cutting into his hands and knees. Trying not to cry out, he scurried over the debris looking for the ill-fitting hard hat.

Reaching up, he discovered that the space above him had narrowed and felt the weight of the mountain bearing down, as if it were settling upon him. He inched forward, moving this way and that, reaching out, touching the face of the wall and grasping the limit of the space around him. He was about to cry out when he saw a flare of a light. After a moment, his eyes began to adjust, and he realized he was seeing the acetylene flare of a carbide lamp against a wall of coal. His Uncle Morgan was there, on his belly under a cut of coal, lying still, head tilted, as if he was listening for something.

Frightened, Asa stopped still, alert, and heard the mountain as he had never heard it from the surface, heaving and turning, laboring under its own weight, shifting its ancient mass somewhere inside its enormous body and releasing hollow groans into the tiny space he occupied. Periodic taps and knocks pierced the dark space, as random as streaks of light in a shower of meteors against the midnight sky.

A vibration rippled through the earth beneath him, whispering for his attention. He saw Morgan push up onto an elbow and place a hand into the black muck where he lay and touch the earth beneath the water. From somewhere down the main shaft behind Asa, a voice echoed. But now the earth seemed still.

"You're late, bud," Morgan said, now aware of Asa crawling from the shadows over fallen plates of shale and piles of coal.

"Couldn't help it, Uncle Morgan. Mama tried to talk me out of it."

"I thought she might. She mad?"

"She's a little bit mad at you."

Morgan snickered. "Little sisters. They can get that way.

You got three ye'self. You'll find out, if you ain't already."

"I reckon," was all Asa could say, glancing about him, looking for something familiar.

"Well, now that you're here," Morgan said, "what do ye think?"

"I ain't likin' it, Uncle Morgan," Asa said, still apprehensive, his voice sounding drawn. He moved closer to his uncle, crawling over the rubble of Morgan's work room, keeping his head low, away from the narrowing roof he seemed unable to ignore a couple of feet above him. His breathing was labored. He coughed, breathed deeply and coughed again.

"Like that fresh farm air, do ye?" Morgan said cheerily.

"Kinda close in here," Asa said. He licked his lips and looked upward, as if trying to comprehend the weight of the mountain above him. The whites of his eyes in the flare of the lamp showed how little he understood.

"It is that, but where else ye a-goin' to make a dollar a day?" Morgan asked. That was the pay Morgan had offered him to go into the mine. "I pick the coal down," Morgan had said last Sunday after church when he pulled Asa away from the rest of the congregation as it gathered outside. He stopped under a broad oak tree behind the little church building. "You break it up and haul it out. Pays by the ton. Six dollars a day if they weigh it honest." Asa had glanced toward the church, looking for Peggy, thinking that real money in his pocket, not just a mess of garden beans for trade in a sack, could change things for him.

"You doin okay, bud?" Morgan asked him.

"I feel like that mule might," Asa said. His face was already streaming sweat and mixing with coal dust from the shaft. Black grime was beginning to appear on his face, but not to the extent that it showed on Morgan. Asa wiped his shirt sleeve across his forehead, smearing the rivulets of sweat.

"Ye goin to look like him, too, when the two of ye start a-pullin' coal out of here," Morgan said. "'But that mule can't shovel coal into a cart like you can. It's what sets us apart from the animals, nephew."

Asa moved closer to Morgan and placed a hand into the water. The water was cold and the coal pebbles under his hand and between his fingers felt gritty and hard. "You goin' to need me tomorrow?" He looked away anticipating the look on his uncle's face for asking the question.

Morgan sat up and looked at him. "I might be able to handle things a couple more days on my own. Let ye think about it a day or two."

Asa nodded, appeared relieved.

"Ye daddy know you're here?"

"I don't know," Asa said. "Momma says he'll find out."

"That worry ye?"

Asa trailed his hand through the water and glanced up again at the roof of coal reflecting the flare of the lamp near his face. It worried him a lot. He had been told by his parents for as long as he could remember that he was never to go into a mine.

"I don't care," Asa said without conviction.

"You're makin' a stand for ye'self, nephew."

"I reckon."

A puff of coal dust suddenly powdered through the flare in the room and a shout from somewhere in the main shaft sent Asa coughing and scrambling to his knees. He looked toward Morgan, who seemed to be considering something.

"Ain't we got to get out of here, Uncle Morgan?" Asa said, starting to move away.

"Hold on," Morgan said. He placed a hand into the black water and touched the wall, appeared to listen. "She's workin' today."

"Who's workin', uncle?"

"Mother mountain," Morgan answered, taking up his pick and turning toward the undercut. "In the mountain or on the mountain, she provides."

Asa watched his uncle strike at the remnants of the vein loosened by the coal shot earlier and wondered about the water pooled where his uncle lay. He knew that water fed the crops and forests and filled the creeks and rivers, but he had never thought much about where water went after it seeped deep into the earth.

"I had to go hunt that sow this morning in the dark," Asa said. "I told Mama she wouldn't wander away too far from the creek. She made me go look anyhow."

"I think she reckoned if you was huntin' a hog you wouldn't be haulin' coal," Morgan said.

"Shoot, she was right where I knowed she'd be," Asa said, energized talking about something familiar. "You know that big chestnut tree up on the hill? Not that little one at the foot of the holler but the one on the other hill. That's where she likes to forage."

Morgan didn't respond. Asa heard the sound of water dripping behind the chunks of Morgan's pick and the flare of the lamp and looked toward the sound. He saw nothing, but he imagined water trickling over roots of trees somewhere above the mine shaft and soaking into the earth, somehow washing down into the mountain in little streams, or hundreds, maybe thousands of tiny channels, loosening the soil as it worked its way toward the mine. He thought the water might make the soil heavy and again sensed the weight of the mountain against him. He inhaled as deeply as he could and wondered where the water went after it fell into the shaft.

"I still got some corn and beans to pick," Asa said.

"You got a while to go," Morgan said between grunts as he picked, the coal beginning to fall away. "First frost is a little ways off. Ye' kale and turnips can take a little cold."

"Cabbage, too."

Asa was silent a while before he spoke. "Daddy wants me workin' on the farm. My sisters do mama's work, and my baby brothers ain't worth much anywhere right now."

Morgan set his pick aside and stood away from his workplace in the water, stooping, avoiding the ceiling. He wiped his hands on his wet pants and picked up his lamp. Shadows danced along the walls with the movement of the flare.

Morgan kicked aside lumps of coal and shale next to

the cart and set the lamp down. He steadied the lamp and squatted in front of Asa. A shadow hid Morgan's face, but Asa could sense resentment.

"It ain't their fault, ye little sisters', them comin one two three just like that. Should'a been a boy among 'em. But there wasn't, and it took ye own life away from ye."

"I reckon," Asa said, looking down, not sure how to take the words his uncle said. He wished he were somewhere else.

"Look at me," Morgan said.

Asa looked into the shadow of his uncle's face. "Your daddy thinks he can get rich makin' dollar money blacksmithin' over at Red Dot if he straps you to that rocky slope he calls a farm. He figures you to plant and harvest and keep up the place. He figures it's a-goin' to make him better off than the other poor devils in the mines that's got nothin' but mine work to live on."

Asa knew Morgan might have been talking about himself.

"You can see what he's up to. But then comes the day when workin' ye daddy's hillside ain't a-goin' to work for you, nephew."

Asa wanted to turn away from the face behind the shadow. Morgan stopped talking, waiting for Asa to say something. But Asa didn't know what to say.

Something seemed to Asa to shift inside the mine. Dust puffed into the lamp's flare behind Morgan and Asa thought he heard the slide of a rock fall somewhere. He became aware of the sounds of the mountain pinging in the outer shaft.

"Sixteen and no chance of a life of ye own," Morgan said, ignoring the mountain. "I seen ye with that pretty little black-haired gal at the church. What's her name?"

Asa felt his heart lurch and blushed, but he knew Morgan couldn't see his face clearly. "Peggy Jewell," Asa said.

"Seen ye with her down at the grocery store, too, sittin' in the shade drinkin' pop."

"That don't mean anything, Uncle Morgan," Asa said.

Morgan said, "What are ye a-goin' to do when ye want to take a wife?"

Asa had thought about it, but he didn't have an answer. He didn't think Peggy would wait for him to get some money, though she had said she would.

When Asa couldn't answer, Morgan placed a hand on his shoulder. "Ye can't take her to ye family's cabin, Asa. Where's she goin' to sleep?"

Asa looked down into the shadows and wouldn't look at Morgan.

"And right off, she'll be housekeeping for your momma and daddy and your brothers and sisters."

Asa knew all that. It was why he had decided to come into the mine.

The mountain around him and his Uncle Morgan standing over him telling him the truth left Asa little space for breathing.

"Ye can make some money with me, nephew," Morgan

said, "and then ye can decide for ye' self."

He picked up a short-handled shovel leaning against the wall and handed it to Asa. "Shovel up what ye can and dump it in here," he said waving a hand at the cart. "What ye can't shovel, pick up with ye hands and what ye can't pick up, ye bust up with this." He handed Asa a sledgehammer. "Fill her up," Morgan said, pointing to the cart, "and lead the mule out. Give this chit to the man at the scale." Morgan gave Asa a small metal coin with a numeral on it. "Unload it, come back here and do it again. Ain't nothin' to it."

Asa watched Morgan drop to his knees into the dark mud and take up his hand pick. He let swing with the pick, and chips of coal went flying into the shadows.

Asa turned to a pile of coal waiting to be shoveled. He worked quickly, knowing to separate coal from slate, driven to get outside onto the surface and into the air. He shoveled and lifted and heaved. Lumps of coal bounced off the insides of the cart and rattled around until the coal began to gather upward along the sides. The difficulty in the mine lay not in the labor, but in the effort required to endure the blackness and the confinement and the knowledge that a mountain of timber and earth, rivers and boulders was above him as he hammered and lifted and heaved coal into the cart.

The movements he made in the mine he had also made on the hillside farm for as long as he could remember. From the first light through the morning mist to the gold light of the evening's close he would grasp a hoe, strike dirt and pull sod, swing an axe, bend to the root and pull until the stump of an oak let go of the earth, hold steady the heavy plow as it cut into the sloping hillside, push the hand plow, turn the rows, bend and place the seed, and then sip cold water from the spring in the shade of the walnut tree as the sweat trickled down his back and cooled his body.

He lifted the last shovelful of coal the cart would hold and tossed the shovel down clattering. The mule shifted and the harness and straps rattled the chains that tethered him to the cart. Asa said softly, "Don't worry ye'self."

Asa's eyes had become accustomed to the illumination of the flare where Morgan worked. He walked along the side of the mule and picked up the strip of leather tied to the bit of a bridle. "Come on, boy," he said flicking the strap, and the mule responded. The feel of the abrupt motion beside Asa and the sounds of the mule and cart and gear were familiar to him.

They made the turn from Morgan's room into the main shaft. Guiding the animal away, Asa could see light in the distance, but he was too far away from the opening to see the green of the hillside across the hollow from the mine exit. He walked steadily beside the mule at the mule's pace, listening to the clatter of its hooves against the shaft floor and the intermittent creaks and squeals of the wheels against the load on the axles.

Shortly, the opening at the exit from the mine came into view and grew larger as Asa and the mule approached the light. He saw gray slag and rock at the entrance and, beyond the heap of debris, a blanket of green on a wooded mountain spur that he remembered rising above a shaded hollow near the operation.

At his back, Asa felt the dark hole where he had left Morgan, and he heard a cry. It was as if Morgan's room were calling out to him. He sensed an invisible force flowing through the roof of the mine shaft and pressing down upon him. His instinct was to drop the bridle lead and run.

Trembling, controlling his impulse to flee, Asa passed through the opening into the light with the mule at his side and breathed deeply, expanding himself, opening his mouth upward toward a snow-white ball of a cloud rimmed in sun gold. He could hear the call behind him, as if the innards of the mountain would not let him go.

"Slate fall," he heard and turned to see a man emerging from the shadows of the mine entrance. "Slate fall," the man repeated, louder. "A big one. It got somebody. He's a goner."

Asa watched, processing the motion around him rather than returning his thoughts into the mine shaft. The weigh man abandoning his scales. Haulers left their mules standing dumb and carts loaded. A blacksmith dropped the foreleg of a mule and ran, hammer in hand. Someone jumped from the driver side of a pickup truck by a slag pile. A tall man in a gray shirt, string tie and knee boots ran with a pistol in a leather holster strapped to his leg. Together they converged and formed spokes around the messenger at the mine entrance.

They stood around the opening, looking into the black hole, shifting their feet, milling about, hands in their pockets, as if to emphasize the lack of a plan. The tall man with the pistol began to point and make motions with his hands, as if issuing directions or offering explanations, but nobody moved toward the opening.

Asa waited for dust and debris to come billowing out of the hole, but nothing appeared. Then he remembered the pools of water where his uncle lay and the trickles of water he heard falling down the mine walls and coal face. Asa thought he should go ask the man reporting the fall if he saw his Uncle Morgan.

But Asa stayed put behind the mule, stroking its face and watching. He tried to imagine what must be happening inside the mountain but could envision only the gray shadows he had seen with his uncle in the flare of the light at the black coal face and the shadowy outlines of crevices in the walls. He wondered if it was truly slate he had seen above his Uncle Morgan.

The men at the opening moved forward. Beyond them, two men emerged from the mine opening. They were carrying something, each swinging an arm as a counterweight, leaning as if they were bearing a heavy load. Asa saw they were carrying a blanket, each man gripping a corner, the load in the blanket between them.

The watchers parted to make room and formed a circle when the blanket was lowered to the ground. A clear view of the blanket was screened by the men milling about the scene, but through a blind of legs, Asa saw a body.

He saw the dark pants and saw that they were like his Uncle Morgan's. He got a brief glimpse of the shirt on the body and wasn't sure. He wanted to leave the mule and the cart of coal he had loaded and run away. But the scene before him stood him still.

The group of men around the body was growing to a crowd and Asa realized that others were emerging from the mine entrance. Without accepting it at first, he saw that his Uncle Morgan was among them.

He stared until he was absolutely certain he was looking at his uncle among those looking at the body. The men began to back away from the blanket, and Asa could see that the hair on the head of the body was light brown. As the body was lifted off the blanket, the head was turned for an instant toward Asa. It looked like Tenney Webb, but the face was misshapen. Asa couldn't be sure. As the body was lifted, the head dropped loosely and dangled like a melon in the corner of a sack. It was Tenney Webb. He went to school with Tenney.

The pickup truck next to the slag pile started up and moved into the crowd gathered around the body. They picked Tenney up off the blanket and lifted him over the side slats of the pickup truck placing him onto the bed, which was too small to hold Tenney flat. One of Tenney's carriers jumped into the bed of the truck and sat against the truck's cab and leaned Tenney back against him. Tenney's head flopped crazily as he was moved into position. The crowd that had followed the body to the truck now stood back as the truck made a turn, boiling up slag dust on its way. Asa wondered where they were taking Tenney. Home, he thought.

Asa had turned to go—maybe to a swift-running creek shaded with trees and fish playing around eddies swirling near a boulder, or to a sunny meadow to watch a hawk soar near the clouds—when he heard Morgan call out to him.

Asa stopped and waited for Morgan to catch up.

"Where ye off to in such a hurry?"

Asa didn't look at his uncle, rather, he looked for a tree to sit under or a log to sit on or a patch of grass to fall down onto. But there was nothing to see anywhere around him but piles of slag and heaps of slate and coal mixed in all the scoured debris overflowing the hillside down to the hollow below. It was all gray and black, the wrong color of mud. He didn't know what to do or where he might go.

"We got to get the load weighed, buddy," Morgan said. "Ye worked hard for it." He put a hand on Asa's shoulder and turned him around to face him.

"But Tenney…" Asa started, but couldn't say the word.

"A slab of slate fell on him, nephew. It wasn't very big, but it was enough to hurt him."

"It killed him, didn't it, Uncle Morgan?" Asa cried out the question.

"I reckon," Morgan said.

Morgan shrugged. "Come on, buddy," he said, laying an arm across his nephew's shoulder. "Let's get this load weighed. Get another load or two and we can go home. I'll go see ye daddy with ye."

The truck carrying Tenney's body had made the turn past the creek and was out of sight. Asa watched the crowd of men breaking up, some walking into the mine, others retrieving their tools where they had left them or walking toward the aluminum tool shed near the entrance.

Asa walked beside his uncle to the cart and the mule that hadn't moved.

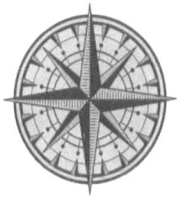

THE BULL

1948

*T*he image I have of the bull is as vivid as a snapshot from a camera. The bull charged with a sudden thrashing out of the brush before I could grasp what was happening. I see clearly the bull at a full stop, head down, horns pointing. Behind the bull is a thick stand of cedars.

A second image follows. Dad, heroically, has advanced toward the bull and is standing right foot forward, left foot back, the saw in his hand whipped to the right from a backhand stroke. Dad advances, the bull turns. In the next image the bull is gone, back into the brush. Dad is explaining that we surprised it. I am not comforted, and I watch my brother throws sticks toward the cedars where the animal disappeared.

I recall, though I have no vivid supporting image, that Dad turned toward us, hands spread to the side, telling us to settle down. I don't remember moving during the incident, so he must have been addressing my brother. I don't know what else my brother might have been doing or if he cried.

Years later, I did not include the story of the bull in my

eulogy for my brother at his funeral service. Instead, I chose to tell only a few simple stories about him from a time in his life that his friends of later times, and even most of his own family, never knew about.

The stories I told were meant to reveal him at memorable moments of his childhood, like when he was four years old, whamming Dad's line gang boss across the knees with a toy baseball bat because he teased me—his big brother. And when, on the afternoon of my eleventh birthday, he took my brand new bike on an excursion up the sidewalk, forming dents with each wreck against the wrought iron fences along the way. The stories I told were well received giving us all a few minutes to think elsewhere, away from the sad occasion before us. I dismissed the story of the bull on that day, though vivid in my memory, for I believed the meaning of the story is not about my brother, but rather about our father, or perhaps even about myself.

When we were kids, Dad would drive us the fifty miles to our grandmother's place about a week before Christmas to walk the hills behind her house to find the fir tree that would stand in our living room for the season. We had to cross a bridge to get there.

A left turn off the bridge and there you were, at grandmother's, on a tiny knoll beside the road overlooking the river. That's the way I remember it: Dad driving the Pontiac and smoking his pipe, me and my queasy stomach in the passenger seat, and my brother standing on the back seat leaning over the front, chattering in our ears about God knows what. I wish I could remember.

At the wooden gate into the yard beyond grandmother's

house, Dad would pull off the road. I'd jump out, the smell of Dad's pipe quickly forgotten. I'd lift the chain off the gate pole and swing it open. Once the Pontiac was through the gate and into the yard, I'd push the gate closed and follow them to the tobacco barn. By the time I caught up, my brother would be out of the car and running around like a wild dog, as Dad described it to his distraction and irritation.

Our mother never minded my brother's enthusiasm for the moment, not even on the day Dad took my brother with him to a routine service check at a power company sub-station and saw my brother with both hands on the very switch on the control panel Dad had told him not to touch. I remember Mom's giggle when he told her. I remember very well that panel with the little flashing red and green lights. On the rare occasions when Dad let me go with him to the sub-station, I would stand obediently to the side, my hands carefully behind my back, fascinated, watching the panel flicker in a colorful array of patterns signaling I don't know what.

To my own distraction and irritation, my cotton head brother at seven years old, as he was on this particular day, could outrun me, then ten. He could throw a rock farther, stand on his head, and to Mother's giggles, pee farther than me over the side of a mountain when we made a rest stop along the road on the way to visit my grandparents and cousins. Dad looked at my brother and these activities in wonder, but looking back, I think he also thought my brother would come to ruin. He didn't until much later, long after a college football career that took him into the game on a cold New Year's night that made Dad proud of him.

Grandmother always greeted us with a hug and a piece of cake. She was a big, muscular woman, already in her eighties on this visit, and her hug for me was, as always, special. On our visits, she let me behave in her house in ways that would get my cousins into trouble. I could sit on her piano stool and bang on the keys as long as I wanted, run up the stairs, jump onto the feather beds, or go into her kitchen for a peanut butter and jelly sandwich. As I recall, my cousins didn't seem to mind the special treatment I got.

The steep hills behind grandmother's house were split with forested hollows bared that day for the winter and revealing the smoky green splotches of fir trees scattered up and down the hillsides within the grey blanket of leafless hardwood trees. These were the well-rounded evergreen trees that were to be examined carefully by critical eyes that would select the one tree to be lashed to the top of the Pontiac, carried to our living room, and smothered in colorful lights, beads, icicles and balls.

Dad told us that, once when he was young, a nest of copperhead snakes was blown off the hillside with dynamite. "They were everywhere," he said, "and a man walked into them before he knew they were under him and all around him." I wondered, when he told us, how anyone managed to set dynamite into a nest of snakes. He said he didn't know, that he wasn't there for the occasion. I asked him to tell me exactly where the nest was. He took his attention away from the tobacco bowl of the pipe he was stuffing with his thumb and waved a hand back and forth. "Up there somewhere," he said. I was not informed nor comforted by his wave that took in the entire mountain.

The way into the hills to find a Christmas tree led past the Pontiac and the tobacco barn, which I remember as most often empty. Besides basic farming tools and a hand plow, there would be bales of hay beneath the loft. If my grandparents ever raised and cured tobacco, it was at a time before my memory. As far as I knew, my grandmother kept only a garden each summer. The garden extended from the fence behind her farmhouse to the little cemetery at the foot of the hollow not far away.

I was told that it was along the garden fence leading to the cemetery that my grandfather died shortly after I was born. The only photograph of him shows a face of angles and edges behind a long white mustache. He had a shock of white hair and a thin, wiry frame. His gaze was directly toward the camera. He fell with a stroke "along here somewhere," my dad told me, waving a hand from side to side.

On all other occasions when I visited my grandmother's house, the cemetery was my demarcation point. I was never told to stay close to the farmhouse, but I understood that I was to stay away from the mountains and off the bridge when I was alone. As I was not an adventurous boy, the instructions were easy to obey. I never perceived my self-imposed boundaries as restrictive.

Behind the cemetery, a narrow hollow gradually rises between two spurs from the mountain to the foot of a steep hillside. Often in winter, the hillsides and hollows were veiled behind a soft white mist, but that day was clear and crisp.

Past the cemetery, we turned left up the hill, Dad in the lead with a handsaw, my brother and me following, Dad's pace respecting the noticeable limitation in my stride due to the infantile paralysis I had contracted as a child.

Except for our sizes and an odd-and-end of clothing, you couldn't tell my brother and me apart: two kids wearing leather jackets, like Dad's; all of us in jodhpurs of the type favored by Dad's line gang; and in high boots laced to the knees. Dad was wearing the fedora he wore climbing power poles toward hot lines. My brother was in his red and black cap with fold-down ear and neck warmers, and I wore my fleece-lined aviator cap. My instructions from Dad were pointed. I was to stay behind my brother and never let him out of my sight.

Much of the hillside had been cleared of hardwood trees, leaving fir and cedar trees like we wanted to stand in our living room. On the way up we passed all of them, disdainful of their ready availability, regardless of their shape. The tree we would have would be in the thick stands of evergreens and hardwoods over the top of the rounded spur, or on another ridge leading down to another hollow, or yet, on a higher ridge. My Dad was a man of these mountains, who followed his own father into these hills and learned the lessons they could instruct, thereby learning what he needed to know to make his own way.

I don't recall us finding the perfect tree or Dad sawing it down, but logic tells me that the tree was found and cut after the incident with the bull.

In the next image, we were moving down the hillside toward the hollow. Dad was in the lead down the steep ravine, perfectly balanced and synchronized with the mountain with my brother bouncing and skipping behind him through the dead leaves. The sun was bright through the tree limbs. I have an image of a tree along the way and of Dad sweeping his hand in its general direction, telling us that he hunted squirrels hereabouts when he was a boy and ate peanut butter sandwiches when he got hungry. I asked him if he leaned against that tree. I recall I needed to know, but he waved a hand again and said he was all around here.

At the bottom, in the hollow, we saw faded wooden stakes driven into the ground in lines following the ravine. On several of the stakes were the letters CCC. Dad stopped and looked at them and was quiet for a while before telling us the lettering referred to a government program from a long time ago. I believed then that Dad was seeing the stakes for the first time. Much later, I would come to understand that Dad never knew before that moment that a platoon of President Roosevelt's army of civilian workers had been assigned duty on my grandparent's property following the Great Depression. It explained Dad's words that day as he looked at the stakes - that "the poor devils" needed government work for food. I now know that Dad must have realized that the President's great welfare project that employed hundreds of thousands of young men and paid them thirty dollars a month to plant millions of trees, build fire roads, and save eroding soil, also saved depressed communities in distant rural areas from extinction.

I never knew why Dad took the side trip and ventured into the hills with his boys on our hunt for a Christmas tree. I've thought that perhaps he wanted to show my brother and me where he spent happy days in his youth, but for all the precision of place he ever revealed, he might just as well have waved an arm in the direction of his boyhood home from his favorite chair in our living room. Now, I think he had something else in mind that day, though he never said what, and I never asked.

The simplest conclusion to draw is that the episode with the bull sent him off the beaten track with us, but I have come to believe that something else came to him that day— the bull that frightened his children and the discovery that his parents, *his family*, as well as the CCC boys, were the beneficiaries of the nation's welfare program of recovery for the nation's poor. I was led inevitably to that conclusion by the next series of images I recall from that day.

My brother and I were on the hill in a clearing among a stand of trees. It was near the brush where we encountered the bull. A cedar tree had been cut and was lying there in front of us. We were alone. I cannot recall, though I have tried to remember over the years, why Dad left us there alone. I had a feeling that I was supposed to do something important, though I couldn't grasp what it was or why I thought so. I simply understood that I was to get the cut tree and my brother off the hill. It was my duty. Once again, I was frightened. My brother was looking at me, saying nothing, waiting.

Together we pulled the tree along the hilltop and around clumps of evergreens. My brother tugged at a branch where Dad made the cut as I pulled at another branch on the other side of the tree. We were both looking into the shadows, fearful of the bull. I was near tears, looking for my Dad.

It seemed forever that we struggled together through the brush, pulling the tree along, eventually moving into another clearing where the hill rounded. At last we could see down to the river and the road well below us, and grandmother's house off to the left.

My brother saw the bull first, below us, a bit to the right and between us and safety. The thing was watching us. We both waited for the bull to charge, and then we saw Dad at the bottom of the hill, standing there, leaning against a fence post, smoking his pipe, watching us. When we didn't move--I didn't know what to do, fearing any movement would cause the bull to come at us--Dad waved at us with a motion to come down. My brother and I yelled for him to come get us, but he didn't. He only waved again for us to come down. We turned away and ran, away from the bull, leaving the tree behind. But Dad called out to me to get the tree and my brother and come down the hill. He stood there, waiting, not coming for us.

I remember standing there on the hill alongside my brother, hesitating, not knowing what I should do, yet understanding that the only thing to do was to go down the hill with my brother and the tree.

I don't remember what was said, but off we went, pulling the tree in jerks and starts, keeping an eye toward the bull watching us as we stumbled and fell, my little brother tumbling and rolling, always ahead of me, bounding with the tree, to the bottom of the hill. At the foot of the hill I saw Dad in profile, looking off, stuffing his pipe, considering what had just happened.

From that moment, my brother continued to tumble

on, away from me, and into his own life of which, mostly, I have not been a part. For the big events—with him his senior year at prep school, with him in his university career in sports, his graduation, his wedding in a distant state, at times with him in his troubles in business—Dad saw to it that I was there with him.

I told none of this at my brother's funeral, leaving the friends that he grew up with and the friends of his later life to know that, early on, he bounded into their lives, and it was they who walked with him through the hills and hollows that were to come.

EMIGRANTS

VIVIAN AND BILLY
1952

*T*he old engine started to whine as Billy floored the clutch and shoved the '41 Dodge panel out of third gear into second. Seated next to Billy, Vivian reached for the passenger door handle and sat up straight.

Around an ascending curve, a bank of exposed sandstone outside Billy's window rose upward and out of sight. The road dipped and then curved above a small hollow of trees below the passenger's side window before curling around another sandstone bend. Lazy curves became sharp angles, then twists and switchbacks as the road rose steadily in dips and turns away from the limestone valley below. Several of the sharp curves up the mountain gave Vivian quick glances back into the valley and across squares of hayfields and grazing cattle. Lines of hazy ridges receded into the distance.

Vivian leaned with each sway of the truck as it cut around bends in the road. From the corner of her eye, she watched Billy's hands glide across the steering wheel. Occasionally his hand moved down to the gear shift, his knees pumping like erratic pistons over the clutch, brake, and accelerator as if he were treading water. His body leaned left and right, flowing with the curves, dancing with the truck. She watched the muscles of his forearm move and work and admired his hands, strong and squared, firm and large for a man as small as Billy, the touch of his fingers on the steering wheel like a caress.

She glanced downward through the tops of trees rising from the mountain's side below her and had a sudden urge to tell Billy to turn the truck around and go back down the mountain, go back into the valley and follow the graceful hillocks with grazing sheep and cattle, back home to their quaint little town of merchants and churches, its shade-tree avenues and fresh air, and its clean schools for Tommy and Patch and little Katy. The urge persisted, but she said nothing and closed her eyes.

Another downward turn into a dip and a tilt upward roused her stomach. Nausea rose to her throat. She opened her eyes and looked ahead toward the road, leveling herself. Billy glanced at her and returned his eyes to the road.

"I'm not going to throw up, Billy," she said. Fifteen-year-old Tommy, their oldest child, throws up in the truck across a mountain, annoying Billy, but she won't, she thought, setting herself, determined.

Settling, she leaned back and folded hers arms against her stomach, as much to acknowledge her nausea as to contain her irritation with Billy. His manly iron stomach against hers that could turn at the thought of fish in a skillet was not fair, and she had never had an answer for it. Tommy got his stomach without having to ask for it.

The road continued turning this way and that. At the crest, the valley was ridges and miles behind them. Sunlight glared through the dusty windshield into her face, burning her eyes. She lowered her eyes and shaded them with her hand, wondering what other affliction might beset her on this trip. She felt Billy's stare and glanced toward him, but he was watching the road.

From behind her in the truck, a mixture of aromas radiated from Billy's tools and laid claim to her stomach. She was aware of a hodge-podge of old electrical motors and motor parts Billy kept at hand: trays of nuts and bolts, compartments of drills and bits, ratchets and rope, pliers and pipe, screwdrivers and screws, rolls of wiring and cutters, and a toolbox of switches, plates and outlets. The vacuum Billy used to clean furnaces with its hoses and brushes radiated dust, or at least the smell of it with a trace of burnt cinders. Rolls of electrician's tape boiling daily inside the truck added a sweet thickness to whatever fragrance the plumber who sold the truck to Billy had left behind. Only God and Billy knew what got tossed now and then into the tray he called the hellbox behind the driver's seat. The burnt tobacco from Billy's pipe touched the back of her throat, and a thin glaze of dampness began to form around her lips.

Her ears popped and the road seemed to narrow and steepen toward the top of yet another mountain. Another wall of sandstone loomed outside Billy's window. Vivian looked down the vertical drop into a deep hollow, the distance to the bottom measured by a momentary glance through the trees to the rusted metal roof of a shack below.

The blind curve ahead set her on edge, and she became angry with herself. She was hatched and weaned on such mountains and roads. Living in the valley had made her soft. She had grown accustomed to her church circle and friends, the main street shops with the friendly clerks in shirts and ties, or heels and hose, and the clean painted benches under the shade trees where she could wait for Katy on a warm afternoon. And that was just fine with her. She bit her tongue and stopped herself from crying.

They were silent most of the way, each keeping thoughts from the other, each waiting for the other to reveal something that might turn things around, or show them something else they might do to save what they had. If there was another way, she couldn't see it. She didn't know what to do. She knew she would stick with Billy, though.

Some time passed, Vivian had lost track of it, when Billy slowed the truck at the top of a mountain and pulled off the road onto a wide shoulder, tires crunching gravel. He stopped the truck and turned off the motor. Engine pops darted to and fro behind the dashboard under the hood in the sudden silence. Vivian's ears felt full, and she moved her jaw about to clear them. Billy stepped out of the truck and reached into his khaki shirt pocket for the can of Half-and-Half tobacco he carried there. A box of matches rattled in his pants pocket.

After a moment, Vivian opened the door and stepped onto the gravel. Cool air touched her face, stirring wisps of brown curls over her forehead. She closed her eyes and listened to the hush. She breathed deeply, expecting the scent of mountain fed oxygen and soil, and at once tasted a familiar arid dust. Billy walked ahead several paces to the edge of the pullover and looked down. Before him was open space. Beyond him was the face of a rough and weathered sandstone mountain ridge. Joining him at the edge of the pullover, Vivian looked down the mountain's side and saw a narrow hollow. At the base of the hollow lay a coal camp.

The camp was pale and colorless, darkened still more by the mountain's shadow. Rows of houses—little more than four-room tarpaper shacks supported on poles and cinderblocks—were strung along both sides of a road. A narrow, swift-running creek flowed behind the row of houses and along the train track at the base of the mountain. The track was little more than a whisper across the creek from the back porch of the houses. On the track, a line of empty cars sat ready to take on coal, the engine up ahead motionless, steaming, waiting. The shacks on the other side of the road backed up to a mountainside that descended to the back doors.

Boards driven into the ground supported the houses. Several houses shared a common coal house, the tenants' buckets arrayed along the coal house walls. Wash tubs hung outside kitchen doors and washing machines took up meager space alongside couches and chairs on porches. Hoes, picks and wheelbarrows leaned against the houses where tiny gardens had been plowed. A way to supplement scant pay. Vivian looked at it and understood it. It all seemed so long ago.

How long had it been? Seventeen years? And that included the time she had lived with Billy's mother on her farm while Billy made his start with the power company, working wherever he was sent with a crew, mostly throughout the mountains to clear right-of-way and string new lines. Billy's sisters living at home had treated her like she was their servant girl, like dirt, really. She had been raised in a coal camp, but that didn't mean she was not as good as them. She had endured their disapproval of her for a year before Billy moved the two of them to a home of their own, a second floor apartment in the home of the nicest people she had ever known, in the town they came to call home.

Down in the camp, the road between the houses was rutted and shaped by trucks passing through the camp daily, back and forth, hauling coal. The edge of the road was graded with dirt and coal shavings. Slag was piled along the creek. A little girl jumped rope in the middle of the road, her little friends turning the rope in a monotonous whirl. Other little girls sat in the road, some holding dolls, awaiting their turn. Behind the row of houses along the creek and in the shadow of the mountain three boys stood in the rushing water and threw river rocks.

Down the road, past the last house, coal miners with their black lunch buckets idled on the steps of a large gray building. Vivian supposed it was the commissary building, where men gathered to while away down time and where women picked up family mail and bought clothes and food on company credit or with company scrip. She pictured herself walking up the steps to purchase what her family would need and paying with the scrip Billy would earn.

Further up the road several men trudged toward the commissary, buckets in hand, their hard, black hats tilted with exhaustion at shift's end. Behind them rose the processor, its conveyers reaching out like appendages from a monstrous grasshopper. A gray haze from the tower lifted into the air between the hillsides.

"Is this our new home, Billy?"

Vivian looked at him. She saw him, still and concentrated, regarding the camp, his face flushed pink. The hot edge of fear she had suppressed returned and nicked her stomach. Billy had never lived like this. He was reared on a farm by farmers who themselves had come from lines of farmers.

"Where's our house?" she asked.

Billy took the pipe from his mouth and cupped it in his way between an index finger and thumb. "Don't know, Viv," he answered.

"You suppose it's that one up there?" she said, pointing up the mountainside to a big white house behind a stand of walnut trees that overlooked the camp. "If it is then there's plenty of room for all of us." She attacked with facetious aggression.

"No, I don't think so," he said, looking at Vivian. "That would be the mine superintendent's house."

"I know that, Billy," she said, her whimsical remarks felt false and wearisome even to herself.

He said, "It might be that we'll have to live in one of those shacks down there til they settle on a place for us."

"The new mine electrician won't get any special treatment?"

"Nope, not right off, I don't reckon'," he answered. "It's a small operation."

Vivian stared at the two rows of houses along the road and the girls jumping rope. Another girl had joined the jumping girl within the arc of the swirling rope. The dress she was wearing looked like it was made from a sack.

Billy said, "You got your own coal house and an outhouse. You got a pump for water and a clothesline. And there's a little ground to grow a garden, if you want to."

He pointed to the other side of the hill toward a smaller house above the shacks, a sizeable house with two floors and a recent paint job. "That's the infirmary."

"The camp has its own doctor?" she said. As she asked the question she wondered if coal camp doctors nowadays made house calls, and if one would walk down the hill in the middle of the night should little Katy wake up with a fever. The memory from her childhood was never far away— her older brother caught in a slate fall, lying on a table in a doctor's office, his head broken and bleeding, his family waiting for him to die, while the doctor went on about other business. There was nothing to be done, the doctor had told them.

"Well, that's where the doctor sets up when he comes calling," Billy said. "That's what they told me anyway. They said a woman works there and keeps it up. She works as a nurse, too, and looks after little hurts that happen. She's kind of like a bookkeeper, too, I was told. Like I say, it's kind of a small operation."

Vivian's stomach fluttered and her courage wilted. She folded her arms across her belly and closed her eyes.

"I don't want to be here," she said.

Startled, Billy gave her a look.

"I don't either, Vivie, but there ain't anything else. This is all the work I can find. I thought we'd decided."

"I don't mean that, Billy. I mean I don't want to be here," she said, and clasped both hands and clutched them to her chest. "Haven't you ever wished yourself out of your own flesh? Just soar away and look back and see your body still there, but you're not?"

Billy said, "Doesn't help to talk like that, Vivie."

Down by the creek the train lurched, startling her and sending the collision of iron couplings through the camp and up the mountainside. The heave of metal went unheeded by the little girls jumping rope and by the boys picking treasures from the creek bed and examining them, as if they were in wonder of them. The train stopped abruptly, the screech and crush of each car's couplers colliding with the next. Billy's face tensed and seemed to recoil, waiting for the next shattering screech.

Vivian let her hands drop to her side and watched him. Until she met him she had lived the life below, and like the little girls on the dusty road and boys standing in the creek, had given as much thought to the sounds of a mine camp as a fish might give to water or a bird to air. From the time she could remember she had swept dirt from a wooden shack, and she had cooked on her feet and scrubbed on her knees with her mother and sisters. Every day she had watched her father and brother come home from the mine, beaten down, bone tired and dirty.

Then on a summer day, when she was seventeen, she

hired herself off as a serving girl at a camp set up by a power company to feed a crew stringing lines across the mountains and had found Billy. He talked different from all the people she knew, and she learned that he had spent a while at a small college. He could read fast and work with numbers, but he didn't have money enough to stay in school. He didn't seem to mind that she had not finished the seventh grade. She learned also that his own life on a farm had been difficult in another way, but he had been young and strong, like her. He had laughed when he told her that he was no better than a mule dragging poles up mountains, as the crew had that summer. She had served him and the sweaty crew beans and cornbread, potatoes and stew for a week, and then she took him home to meet her family. The look on his face when he saw where she lived had hurt, but he had wanted her and she wanted him.

"The day's getting on, Vivie," Billy said. "We ought to go on down there."

"You saw it when you took the job, Billy. We don't need to see it together."

"You need to see it for yourself. Stand on the ground." He shrugged slightly, as if it really didn't matter.

"They all look the same," she said.

Billy touched a match to his pipe bowl and turned his head away from her, masking his broken pride.

"We can't go back and change things," he said.

"Too late for that, all right," she said.

She knew it in her heart as well as in the checkbook they

shared, and her heart lurched like a loaded coal train. A flare of heat washed over her, just as it did the day Billy came home and told her the power company was transferring him. She had felt a hard thump in her heart and had gone weak, nearly fainting.

She couldn't understand how it could be, nor did she realize the full meaning of what Billy had told her. Her ignorance had protected her. After all, Billy's job with the power company had changed before, while the little town where they had lived for fifteen years had not changed. Whatever had come his way, the town and their new home never changed. Billy cleared right-of-way, strung transmission lines, got called out in rain and snow and ice, climbed poles, serviced transformers and insulators, replaced downed lines in storms, restored power, read deeds and found property for right of ways. More things than she knew to say. In all that, she herself prepared their food, kept their home and raised their children in a home she could believe was a gingerbread house in a little toy town.

Billy's new job was to have been on-site electrician for a large coal mine that was serviced by Appalachian Power in West Virginia. He would be the mine's electrician, maintaining electrical services provided by the power company to the huge mine. He was to live at the mine on mine property. He was told the coal company provided a school building for children from first grade through high school. There was a medical office staffed by a full-time nurse and serviced by a doctor four days a week. He was told the mining company had made available a building for religious services of varying denominations. The new assignment wasn't thought by anyone to be a promotion. Billy never knew how he was chosen from among all the linemen available in the valley district.

Vivian thought Billy's boss was behind the transfer, but it was never clear if Billy's boss had recommended Billy to the district supervisor. Though Billy's foreman was crude and rough spoken and quick to take offense at slights, Billy couldn't think of anything specific he himself might have done to cause the transfer, nothing more than any other employee might have done.

Billy had appealed to his foreman to understand that he couldn't move his family away, just like that, or take his kids out of their schools. And there was the new house they had borrowed the money for and built.

Vivian had gone about her own business, safe in her new home, baking cakes and pies for the children and preparing Billy's breakfast and packing his lunch. She had found diversion and comfort in their church and her prayer circle. Billy had found a diversion in the church choir. Their oldest child, Tommy, named for her fallen brother in the mine, surprised them with his interest in school and the activities it afforded. He seemed to flower in the high school. Vivian had found refuge from a mounting fear in the company of the mothers of the friends of their other son, Patch, and daughter Katy.

Then that horrible moment came. She was moving about in her kitchen, preparing the pots and strainers, the spoons and stirring paddle, the sugar and spices for Billy to use to make the season's apple butter. She was looking out the kitchen window, admiring the fall colors on the hillside across the avenue and studying the brick fireplace Billy had lain to cook the apples, when it all rose to the surface, the certain knowledge that they were going to lose their home and that the children's lives would be turned on end. She would be moving Katy, Patch and Tommy into a coal camp.

That day, Tommy had had come upon her unexpectedly and found her heaving in sobs on the front porch. Gaining some control, she had tried to reassure him, but she could tell that Tommy didn't believe her. She tried to explain a lie to him, that her shoulder was burning with pain and that she would see a doctor when his father came home. Tommy, frightened and confused, had wandered off, and she was grateful.

Tommy didn't tell his father what he saw, but Vivian had made a doctor's appointment anyway, to cover herself. In the doctor's office, she learned that her right shoulder was actually in early stage bursitis. She had scrubbed too many floors, the doctor had reckoned jokingly. Tommy seemed to accept her new story, but he had changed toward her. She thought he would not ever forget seeing her the way he found her on the porch. From that moment, worry seemed never far from his face, and he set himself apart in the house and kept company with his friends and his activities.

Below, in the camp, the train lurched again, the sound of the collision down the line of cars shrieking throughout the hollow and up the mountain. Billy was gripping his pipe and staring into the camp.

She thought that if it weren't for the children, she and Billy could have taken the assignment to the mine. After all, she was raised in a mining camp, and before they met, Billy had been a carefree spirit, she thought, working wherever he was assigned, as if the company had done him a favor. He was a good worker, a trusted man good for his word, a skilled lineman who had come to feel comfortable in courthouses with men in coats and ties. With little thought, they could have taken the assignment and looked ahead five years or so to a promotion of some kind.

One evening, sitting together on the front porch, Katy in the house playing pretend, Patch on a chase of fox and hounds somewhere on his bicycle, Tommy off with friends, they had made the fateful decision. They agreed that Billy wouldn't take the assignment into West Virginia, and that they didn't need the power company. They made up their mind that Billy would buy a truck and start an electrical contracting business of his own. In the darkness, within the soft sounds of night, it had all sounded so good.

They could say they had tried, but work had not come Billy's way, and the contracting business never got off the ground. There were no contracts to be had to wire houses or businesses or barns, or whatever, for a simple reason. Two other established electrical contractors were already in town, and that didn't leave much work for a new man setting up. Like two innocent children—or fools, she thought—they hadn't counted on that. Though Billy had done his best, the work he had been able to find was down in basements cleaning furnaces, or else picking up house lamps and kitchen fans at back doors to bring home for repair. It wasn't enough.

Friends from the church came forward with offers of assistance—Bill, who owned a department store; Pete, a postal worker; Sam, who delivered bread; a grocer. But there was little they could do for a man whose only skill was working with electricity. Mr. Orren, president of the bank and who sang with Billy in the church choir, took Billy aside one morning in the few minutes between church school and church service. He invited Billy to come to the bank to discuss a loan, if Billy thought that would help. Mr. Orren's kindness touched Billy, but the offer was one that he could not accept without the hope of being able to repay the loan and the kindheartedness of Mr. Orren. The loan would have been charity and the inevitable default an embarrassment and a humiliation.

Now there they were, she thought, standing on an overlook, staring down a mountainside into a coal camp where Billy had managed to find a job doing the only work he knew how to do. The pay was little better than miners' pay.

"We're almost out of money," he said. "And I can't find work," he waved a hand at the scene below, "'cept this."

Her throat tightened, as if it was news coming as a surprise.

"We got some money," she said. "Winter's coming. People need their furnaces cleaned." Saying it, she knew she couldn't look at Billy. She couldn't look into his face that had once carried such honest pride as a man. Her torment and his was all she could bear.

"Nobody's calling me, Vivie. I'm having to knock on doors and ask if they've got work for me." He looked at her and his hazel eyes were moist and bright. "It's like I'm begging."

She turned toward the side, as if surveying the scene before them, hoping Billy couldn't see her starting up. She absently pursed her lips before looking at him.

"You know we can't let our children live here like this," she said.

"I think maybe they'll be fine," Billy said, looking away as if interested in the house on the hillside, a move that didn't fool her. He sometimes said things like that to her, as if he was not in on a problem. Billy drew from his pipe, propped a boot on the stump and leaned on an elbow. He appeared confident and at ease, a facade that came naturally to him, and she drew some comfort from it. It was a good reason why she loved him.

"Katy needs a room of her own," she said.

"Can't she can stay in our room?"

"She's nine and she needs a room of her own…and so do we…and so does Tommy and Patch."

She didn't expect an argument, and Billy didn't offer one.

"Tommy's got a girlfriend," she said.

"Tommy's got a lot of girlfriends," Billy answered. "I've had a talk with him. He can come see me if he has any questions. He knows that."

Vivian stared at Billy for a moment, but Billy didn't take notice.

"He's moon sick over the Buckley girl, and his heart's breaking because she's away for the summer."

Billy looked at Vivian and stared.

"Buckley? The lawyer?"

Vivian nodded. "Our first child is in love, Billy."

"He's reaching," Billy said, returning his pipe to the corner of his mouth. He looked away toward a far mountaintop. Vivian followed his line of vision to a series of power line poles rising along a cleared right-of-way toward the crest of the hazy ridge.

He said, "Viv, I don't think Tommy knows about any of this."

"He suspects something," she said, thinking back to the afternoon he discovered her crying on the porch. "I believe he thinks there's trouble between you and me."

"How could he be oblivious?"

"He's a dreamer," she said.

Billy nodded. "He's that, all right. Cleaning a furnace with me, it's like he's off somewhere in fantasyland. I've wondered what he's thinking about."

She knew that about her oldest child. "He'll die down there," she said.

Billy was quiet for a while.

"And momma's little favorite will be the cause of a lot of trouble," he said, looking into the hollow.

"I love all my children, Billy," she said. But, yes, Patch was a troublemaker. A bright-eyed, smiley faced, charming little tough guy who took things apart and never put them back together again.

139

She pictured Katy jumping rope with the little girls and couldn't make it seem real. What she could see was Katy running off into the hills with one of the boys wading in the creek. Katy, like herself, growing up in a coal camp.

"Billy," she started, but then she stopped, not finishing what had come to mind. Billy's name hung in the air, waiting for the words to follow.

"I know, Vivie," he finally said.

They were both silent for a while, watching the shadows lengthen across the camp and the sunlight brighten the distant mountain with effortless clarity.

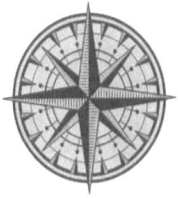

THE BONES FROM
THE CAVE

1996

"Peg, listen to this."

Bud McGuire sat in his leather recliner reading the A-section of the Sunday edition of the Orlando Sentinel. Peg, his wife of 48 years, was seated nearby at her personal computer entering data, concentrating on the names, dates, and minutia she'd uncovered in a recent genealogical search, her current passion. Peg taught an evening adult class in genealogy at the local branch library, which added negligible income to their comfortable retirement—Peg from a university teaching career, Bud from a city homicide division.

Bud glanced toward Peg, who had turned to look at him, adjusted his wire rim glasses and read aloud. "It says here 'Scientists say a skeleton found in a cliff-side cave this spring by climbers scaling the sheer walls near The Gap, a natural scenic formation in Virginia's mountainous southwestern region, is from a period more recent than locals earlier claimed.'"

He tipped the newspaper and looked again at his wife.

"Peg, I know that area. I spent the war there."

"Um-hum," Peg said, "Guarding prisoners."

"Nazi prisoners," Bud said. He returned to the newspaper and continued reading. "'A regional historian had speculated that the bones belonged to a legendary Indian thought to have been wounded in a skirmish with mountain settlers more than 200 years ago.'"

"Now listen to this," Bud said. "'An anthropologist says the bones are probably no more than 50 or 60 years old.'"

Bud looked up. "I was there in forty-four and forty-five," he said and buried his face once again into the newspaper.

Peg turned away from her computer, more curious about Bud's interest in the article than in the content of the story.

"'The remains have not been identified, and Owens County Sheriff's Deputy Ted White said they may never know who the skeleton belonged to. White says the sheriff's office has no idea why the skeleton was in a small opening beneath the edge of a cliff with a sheer drop of a thousand feet to the rocky banks of a river below.'"

Bud laid the newspaper down on his lap and looked at Peg, something on his mind.

"This is about that German prisoner that got away, isn't it, Bud?"

"Nazi prisoners brought to the United States for incarceration fled, now and then, Peg, but they never got away. They could walk away from a work detail if they felt lucky, but they'd be captured before they got very far along. That's the way it was."

"But yours got away."

Bud nodded and lowered the newspaper to the floor. "The date was June 6, 1944. About a half dozen prisoners got out of the compound after lights out. Normandy was being invaded and there I was, chasing runaways over the mountains. We got 'em all by the next evening. All except one. Dietrich Theodore Weissmann. Dieter Weissmann. We must have looked under every bush up every hollow on Pine Mountain. We never caught him, but I never believed he got away."

"Why would you believe that? I mean given the fact that prisoners never got away."

"Because Dieter had a hip wound that left him too lame to do much more than menial labor. I don't believe he could have walked any distance over that rough country, much less climb steep mountains to avoid capture."

"Maybe he stole a car."

"Maybe...and maybe he didn't have to steal a car."

"He had friends on the outside?" Peg said skeptically.

"Dieter was a charmer. He used to flirt with the girls working the lunch kitchens where the prisoners were fed when we had them out working the hills. They thought he was handsome."

"Was he handsome, Bud?"

"How would I know, Peg? But, I guess you might say being tall, blond, and blue-eyed didn't hurt him where the girls were concerned."

"A young girl's flirting shouldn't be taken seriously."

"Maybe not, but the mountains isolated the families there. And existence was meager. Coal mining was a difficult way to make a living. Young people saw the prisoners as exotic and fascinating."

"So, you think someone might have helped him escape?"

"I began to suspect that was possible. One girl in particular was infatuated with him, and bold about it. She couldn't have been more than seventeen years old, if that. It crossed my mind then that she could have hidden him away somewhere in the hills. But then, I learned she'd left town for a job. She got out. She was a little beauty. Vicey Preece was her name."

"You remembered, Bud. How sweet."

"Can't help it, Peg. Allowing those prisoners to escape while I was head of the MP unit attached to Camp Pike to guard them was bad enough, but letting Dieter get away was a mark against my record."

"Looking back, Bud, can you see that it seems a bit romantic? A young girl smitten by the handsome, forbidden warrior?"

Peg, whose university career and current genealogical research inundated her with endless facts, found pleasure in imagining the richness that might have been the true lives behind the dates and stark land deeds of her ancestral searches.

"It was foolishness, Peg. Those prisoners were brought to Camp Pike to labor in the hollows of the mountains, the same as Franklin Roosevelt's CCC boys worked in other depressed areas, but it brought them into contact with the locals. Some of those people who'd already lost family in the war wanted them dead. Banner Preece was one of them."

"The little beauty's father?"

"That's right," Bud said. "His oldest son, Vicey's brother, was killed a few months earlier at Anzio, leaving Banner and his wife with Vicey and two boys. Banner wanted all the prisoners dead. He said so, too, that day the lieutenant decided to stop the bus and take the prisoners shackled into Banner Preece's store to buy cigarettes. Dieter asked Banner the price of a shotgun and Banner answered that it just cost him his life. I swear to you, Peg, if the lieutenant hadn't intervened, Dieter would have died where he stood."

"I see. Now you're thinking the skeleton found in the cave might belong to Dieter."

"It's a stretch, but maybe I am, Peg. Or maybe I just can't let it go."

Peg, a tall woman with an agility of motion that belied her 72 years, stood up and walked to the table beside Bud's recliner. "Let's just see about that, Bud McGuire." She picked up the telephone and dialed information for the area code and number to the office of the sheriff of Owens County, Virginia. She dialed and held the handset to Bud.

Bud smiled and put the receiver to his ear.

The duty officer answering the call introduced himself as Sheriff's Deputy White, who told Bud the sheriff had been ill and was not in his office that Sunday morning.

Bud said, "Deputy White, I'm Bud McGuire, calling from Orlando. I'll come straight to the point. I want to describe for you the person whose skeleton was found in the cave at The Gap not long ago. I think you'll agree that the skeleton belonged to a Caucasian; early- to mid-twenties; about six feet, one inch tall; with a wound to the hip bone on the right side. Now, Deputy White, if you have reason to believe I might be able to assist you in your investigation of this homicide, my wife and I will be happy to drive to Owens County and talk with you."

Bud waited with the receiver to his ear then looked up at Peg and grinned. "Peg, I think the deputy has been rendered speechless."

"The cave where the skeleton was found is about sixty feet down the face of the cliff," Deputy Ted White said to Bud, pointing over the safety rail of The Gap's State Line Overlook. The overlook stood atop a sheer wall with a breathtaking drop nine hundred sixty feet to the cliff bottom, where the mountain sloped further downward to the Russell Fork River. Over time, the rapid Russell Fork had cut the gorge that formed the spectacular view Bud was admiring once again after more than a half century. The view across the canyon was into the mountains of Kentucky.

Bud pointed downward to the right to a thin ribbon of road. "As I remember, that road is leading off this mountain top to DuPuy, just across the state line. Camp Pike was about ten miles beyond Dupuy. That's how far Weissmann would have had to travel with a painful hip wound and a limp to get to this cliff side."

"My opinion, Mr. McGuire, is that your prisoner could have caught a ride on the back of a coal truck or somebody's pickup. He somehow got down to that cave to hide out while the search for him was hot, and couldn't get himself up the cliff wall when it was time to go. He laid in that cave and starved to death. That is, if the bones from the cave belong to your prisoner."

Bud said that the deputy's theory was reasonable, given that Weissmann came from Germany. Climbing experience Dieter could have gained there might have led him to choose the cave in the mountain as a temporary haven.

White had met Bud earlier that morning in the Rhododendron Lodge and Restaurant overlooking The Gap, where Bud and Peg had reserved a room before their arrival the evening before. White had asked Bud to call him Ted but had politely declined to refer to 77-year-old Bud by his first name. Both men shared a military history, both serving in the Military Police, Ted White also serving combat duty in Vietnam. White, now in his fifties and fit, had retired from the military to his hometown of Monroe near The Gap, taken a part-time job with the county sheriff's office, and now, Bud suspected, had ambitions for the high office of sheriff.

"The citizens of this area held a lot of animosity toward those prisoners," Bud said. "Especially Banner Preece. Banner threatened to kill Weissmann on one occasion. He'd already had a son killed fighting Nazis in Italy. His daughter was seen on several occasions flirting with Weissmann. And Preece had a temper."

White looked across the deep gorge. "Banner Preece lost

another son in that war. His boy Adron was killed in the Battle of the Bulge several months after Paul died at Anzio. It was told when I was young that Banner Preece vowed to stand at his door and die before he would allow the military to take his youngest boy, Jessie. Mercifully, the war ended as Jessie came of age. Those were hard times, I think, Mr. McGuire."

Bud remembered the black wreaths that hung on front doors of homes in the mountain towns during the war, symbols of loss and grief endured in silence and isolation. But Banner Preece was not silent.

"Ted, I'd like to ask your permission to talk to any people who might have been here at that time and who might remember something. I'd like to get this off my chest."

"Banner Preece died thirty years ago."

"His daughter, Vicey, whatever happened to her?"

"She lived in Ohio for a while."

"I mean now. Where is she now?"

"She's living here," White said, looking down toward a miniature train exiting a tunnel alongside the river. "She's a widow, seventy-three, living under her married name. She'll be no trouble to find."

Vicey Preece, now Vicey Metters, lived a good life in a little white house by the side of the road, a winding, eight-mile asphalt surface up the mountain from Monroe to The Gap overlook. A variety of brightly colored flowers grew in beds in a freshly cut and trimmed lawn that extended to a shaded back yard on the edge of a steep slope down the mountain. The living room inside her home was decorated with colored glass and pottery and trinkets of coal and porcelain. Bud sat in a soft chair with a bright green and yellow covering. Peg sat with Vicey on a colorful matching couch on the other side of a glass-topped coffee table displaying a fan of home and garden magazines and religious reading material.

Ted White had called ahead and requested an appointment with Vicey for Bud and Peg. Vicey Metters, whose deceased husband had been the chief administrator of a local bank, seemed pleased to have out-of-town visitors. She poured tea from a silver service and had laid cookies in a matching tray. Peg and Vicey exchanged pleasantries, Peg inquiring about local genealogical issues, Vicey telling Peg that early county court records could be patchy, given a fire during earlier times, but that court personnel were usually very helpful.

Vicey appeared to Bud to be happy. He could see in her countenance a trace of the seventeen-year-old girl he had once interviewed. Vicey did not appear to recognize Bud.

"Mrs. Metters," Bud said, following introductions, "we met, you and I, a long time ago, back in 1944, following the prisoner escape from Camp Pike. I was a sergeant then, a military policeman, stationed there to help guard the place. You might remember I interviewed you about what you might be able to tell me about one particular prisoner. Dieter Weissmann."

For a minute, Bud thought that it would have been better had he not bothered Vicey Preece Metters with his old problem, for her face drained of color and her expression

153

froze. Her eyes that had sparkled with light only moments before now stared through him, dull as the pale porcelain figurines on the table beside her.

Bud waited for Vicey to gather herself, but Peg spoke up. "Perhaps we shouldn't have come, Vicey."

"No, please," Vicey said, "I'm all right. I thought I had put those days behind me."

Bud waited a moment more before going on. "You're aware, I'm sure, of the skeleton discovered in the cave here at The Gap."

Vicey nodded and folded her hands around the tissue she had used to wipe her eyes.

"We won't know for sure until some kind of corroborating evidence can be found, but I'm convinced that the skeleton belongs to Dieter Weissmann."

Vicey's reaction was as if Bud had reached across the coffee table and slapped her face. Her head jerked and she covered her face with her hands. Bud thought she was going to faint.

Peg spoke. "Bud, please go outside. I'll see to her and be out shortly."

"No," Vicey whispered, shaking her head from side to side. "No," she repeated. Bud sat still and looked at Peg for guidance. Peg put a hand on Vicey's shoulder and patted her.

In a few moments Vicey looked up and said, "I have to know what happened to him. Please tell me."

"Nobody knows, Vicey. Scientists say the bones are from

that time period. The skeleton matches Dieter Weissmann's characteristics."

"Do you mean he never left?" Vicey asked, a look of bewilderment on her face.

"It looks that way."

"How did he die?"

"I don't know. It's possible he starved to death. And we don't know how he got into the cave down the face of that cliff."

"Did he die alone?"

"It appears he did."

Vicey wiped her eyes and declined the cup of tea Peg lifted for her.

"Vicey, I need to ask you about the last time you might have seen or talked to Dieter."

"I don't really remember. It was probably at Mac's Lunch Room where I worked and the prisoners sometimes were fed after working on the mountain." She thought a minute. "Yes, I do remember. I was serving one evening the prisoners were brought in. I set his plate down in front of him, and he laid a silver ring beside the plate. It matched the one he wore. He told me to take it in case he never saw me again."

As if to prove her words, she stood and disappeared into another room. When she returned she held a silver ring in her hand and laid it on the coffee table in front of Bud.

"Did you ever see him again?"

"No."

"Do you have any idea how Dieter Weissmann might have gotten onto that mountain, or what might have happened to him after he escaped from Camp Pike?"

Vicey thought for a moment and then answered. "I don't know the answers to those questions, Mr. McGuire, but I do know that my father forbade me from leaving the house for several weeks after the breakout. I was confined to the house while my father took my little brother Jessie into the mountains every day. My father said he wanted to find a Nazi and show Jessie how to kill people who kill family."

"Do you think he found and killed Dieter Weissmann?"

"I didn't think so at the time. When the military never captured him, I assumed he got away. Jessie came to hate the Nazis the same way my father did. He told me Dieter was never coming back. I asked him how he knew. He said it was because Dieter was a Nazi. Those were his words. Now, I'm not sure what to think."

"I'm sorry to have troubled you this way, Mrs. Metters, but I had to ask."

"It's all right. You've answered a question for me. I always wondered if Dieter got back to his home." She looked at Bud, her expression settling for the first time since she'd heard the news about Dieter Weissmann. "After all these years, Mr. McGuire, Dieter was on the mountain. Just up the road. All the time."

Bud and Peg were eating a breakfast of cereal and French toast by the restaurant window overlooking the canyon toward the sheer walls of The Towers, a vertical rock peak that formed as the rushing Russell Fork River wove its way through the Cumberland Mountains.

"You know, don't you, Bud," Peg said, "that Vicey is still very much in love with Dieter Weissman."

"The man's been dead fifty-five years."

"I would still be in love with you if you'd left me years ago."

Bud looked at The Towers and forked a bite of French toast.

"I don't want you going, Peg," Bud said.

"I've already ordered a rental car, Bud. I'm going," Peg said gently.

Peg told Bud the evening before, as they sat on the porch of their room listening to the sounds of the night above the canyon, that she had rented a car to drive herself to the county seat. She wanted to visit the courthouse there and examine old records, perhaps finding use for the material in her class at the library.

"Well, I don't like it," Bud said. "These mountain roads are winding and treacherous."

"That was fifty years ago," Peg said patiently. "Surely the roads have been widened to accommodate modern cars."

Bud hoped so because he knew Peg well enough to know that she was making the trip whether he liked it or not.

White told Bud that Jessie Preece could be found almost any hour of the day at The Tree, a liquor joint a few miles outside of Monroe on the road to Keen Mountain. The Tree was the kind of rough mountain watering hole Bud remembered from his year of duty at Camp Pike. He found Preece sitting alone at the bar, bony legs crossed, a bottle of beer in his hand, his overalls and cotton shirt needing a wash. In his early seventies and nearly toothless, Jessie Preece was a pathetic sight.

Bud thought about the approach to take with Preece. Assuming that Weissmann could have been murdered and his body placed in the cave, and having only Banner Preece as a suspect under that hypothesis, Bud figured to be direct.

"Mr. Preece, my name is Bud McGuire," he said, seating himself on a stool alongside the small man. "I was a military policeman at Camp Pike back in the forties. I'd like to ask you a few questions."

Preece drew a swallow of beer and looked away from Bud.

"I guess you've heard about the skeleton found in the cave at The Gap," Bud said easily.

"Who ain't," Preece said, and took another swallow.

"I have this idea, Mr. Preece, that the skeleton belongs to one of the prisoners who broke out of the camp back in forty-four. Do you remember anything about those days?"

Preece looked toward Bud for the first time, taking a measure of Bud, then returned to his bottle. "What makes you think I'd know anything about that?" Preece said, his voice nasal with an unmistakable mountain inflection.

"Your sister Vicey said so."

Preece looked at Bud with the unfocused gaze of an alcoholic. His bushy eyebrows needed trimming.

"Wha'd she say?" Jessie asked, still staring at Bud.

"She said on the night of the escape and for a week afterward, while she was restricted to home, you and your dad went hunting for prisoners."

"That's a lie," Jessie said, making a face that Bud couldn't interpret.

"What happened, Jessie?"

Preece looked at Bud warily, then held up his nearly empty bottle for Bud to see. Bud motioned to the large man with a full beard behind the bar.

A cold bottle of beer was delivered to Preece, and Bud said, "Tell me what you remember."

Preece's suspicious look turned to apprehension. "Nazis killed my brothers."

"So, you and your father went hunting for them."

Jessie didn't answer. Bud asked, "Did your father kill a prisoner, Jessie, and put him in the cave to hide the fact?"

"Ain't 'cause he didn't try. Broke his heart when Paul got killed."

"Are you saying your father did not kill that German prisoner?"

"I ain't sayin' anything."

"But the two of you went hunting for prison runaways. Why did you say it was a lie when I asked you? Are you playing games with me, Jessie?"

"That wadn't the lie," Jessie said. "The lie was Vicey sayin' she didn't go out that night. Daddy tried to make her stay home, but she ran out of the house. I follered her."

"Where did she go, Jessie?"

"Got in her girlfriend's car. I follered in my friend's car 'till she got outta town and started up the mountain toward Dupuy."

Dupuy was fifteen miles across the mountain from Monroe. At the top, halfway between the two towns, was the entrance to The Gap overlook.

"Where did she go, Jessie?" Bud repeated.

"Don't know. I went home. Me and dad had some Nazis to hunt."

Bud heard the footsteps coming down the walkway and knew Peg was returning to the lodge from her day trip to the Owens County seat. The afternoon was growing toward evening, and he had been worried. Peg seemed to Bud to breeze into the room, fresh as if she were just now leaving for the morning, and said, "You need to be sitting down, Sugar. I've got something to tell you."

Bud sat and watched Peg withdraw machine copies of papers from her briefcase. "While I was rummaging about the courthouse I decided to see what I could find out about Vicey. Bud, she didn't marry Vernon Metters until she was twenty-eight years old, in nineteen fifty-five."

"Not unusual to marry late."

"But very interesting because five years later the nineteen sixty census shows the Vernon Metters household with three children, a three-year-old, a four-year-old, and a fifteen year-old boy."

"Metters already had a kid when Vicey married him."

"No. I checked back ten years earlier to the nineteen fifty census and found Vicey Preece living as the sole adult in a household with—listen to this—a five-year-old boy. Bud, Vicey gave birth in nineteen forty-five."

"What does the birth certificate say about birth date, or name?"

"There's no record in the courthouse of Vicey's having a child. So, I went through the nineteen fifty-five issues of the local weekly newspapers looking for Vicey's wedding announcement. I found it. Vernon Metters was a vice-president of a local bank at the time. The announcement mentioned Vicey's five-year-old child by name and birth date. Birth date was March 5, 1945."

Peg paused to let Bud do the math. "The child's name, Bud, was Theodore White."

Bud stared through Peg while the information processed, then looked at her to see if her conclusion was the same as his own.

"Dieter Theodore Weissmann," Bud said. "Peg, Ted

White is Dieter Weissmann's child."

"Yes, Bud. Weissman, weiss, white in German. Vicey must have been able to meet with Dieter alone. Afterward, learning that she was pregnant, she went away to have her baby, giving it, essentially, Weissman's name. Then she returned here and waited for him, but he never came back. She didn't know that he never left."

Bud thought a minute. "Peg, I have to talk to Vicey Preece again. I know Banner Preece killed Weissman. I just have to prove it somehow. Want to come along?"

Peg convinced Bud that Vicey must be handled gently. After all, Peg said, Vicey was about to learn that it was her father who probably killed the man she loved enough to share an intimate, if desperate, moment with. Bud said he thought Vicey's moment was the foolish act of an immature and lovelorn teenager. Peg pointed out that, however it all came about, Ted White was now involved, and neither Bud nor Peg knew if White knew his own history. Also, Peg pointed out, the murder, if indeed it was murder, would have to be investigated and made public. It was clear to Peg, and finally to Bud, that the lives of Vicey Metters and her son, Ted White, were about to change. Peg called Vicey, who said she was expecting them.

A sheriff's cruiser was parked in Vicey Metter's driveway when Bud and Peg arrived after dark. The porch light was turned on. Vicey met them at the door and invited them inside, where Sheriff's Deputy Ted White was in uniform, standing by the couch. The expression on his face was flat, controlled, Bud thought. White's greeting was not warm. Bud hesitated only an instant, then took the same chair that Vicey had offered him on his previous visit. Peg hugged Vicey and sat in another chair beside Bud.

"You already know my son, Ted," Vicey said, sitting on the sofa across from Bud and Peg. She took her son's hand, pulling him gently toward her. He sat down beside her, the leather holster holding his heavy service revolver brushing against the fabric of his uniform.

"Ted knows about his father" Vicey said, not waiting for Bud and Peg to tell their reason for wanting to speak with her. "After you left I thought about what you told me and I was able to come to a decision. I couldn't allow my son to continue believing the lie I had led him to believe all these years, that he was the son of an American serviceman who went off to war and left me with a child."

She held her son's hand with both of hers and looked more to him than to Bud or Peg when she spoke. "The story I told was that I left and met and married a young man by the name of White, who went away to war and was killed. It was a common story, easy to tell, and easy to believe. I did my son and the memory of his father an injustice. An insult, really, for which I beg his forgiveness."

It appeared to Bud, who was studying Ted White's face, that the forgiveness Vicey sought from her son was there for her, but Bud was unable to decipher Deputy White's mood.

"There's still the matter of how Weissmann died and how

he came to be in that cave," Bud said.

White stirred, but Vicey held his hand tightly.

Bud continued, "Your brother Jessie told me you disobeyed your father and left the house the night of the escape. He said he saw you get into a car and go up the mountain toward Dupuy. He said he followed you a short distance out of town and then returned home to get a gun and go hunting the escaped prisoners with his father."

Vicey closed her eyes a minute, more in debate than in recollection, Bud thought.

"It's true my father hunted for the prisoners and wanted to kill them. He wanted my little brother Jessie to take revenge for the death of Paul, but it is not true that my little brother returned home after following me only a short distance that night."

"What happened? Mrs. Metters."

"When Dieter left the silver ring for me on the lunchroom table, it was his signal to me to meet him at the overlook on the mountain. We had agreed on that earlier."

Vicey pointed to the silver ring she had shown Bud and Peg two days before. It was still lying on the coffee table in front of her. Ted White stared at it coldly, his face reddening.

"He had told me that if he ever showed me the ring again, it would be a signal that he could get away for a while without being seen. I know now I was a naive child for believing a prisoner might leave and yet somehow return to his place of detention, but I truly loved Dieter," Vicey said, looking at White beside her.

"He hoped that I could arrive with my father's car, so that we might drive someplace, anyplace. I didn't care. I understand now that he probably wanted the car to use to get away."

"Yes, ma'am," Bud said gently, "using you as a hostage."

"I hope that is not true, Mr. McGuire. Anyway, I called a friend who had a car, who took me to what is now the entrance to The Gap overlook. She went on to Dupuy and was to return in an hour or so, and wait for me. But Jessie had followed us, and he followed me to the overlook."

"That's rough country," Bud said. "Wasn't that dangerous? You could have fallen over one of the cliffs in the darkness."

"We grew up here," Mr. McGuire. "We climbed over those mountains and down the cliffs and ledges, just as our ancestors had done before us on that same mountain."

"Jessie saw you with Dieter, didn't he?" Mrs. Metters.

"Yes, but I didn't know he did, not for a couple of months anyway, until it was becoming obvious that I was pregnant. That's when Jessie told me my Nazi boyfriend would never come back for me."

"Was it Jessie who killed him, Mrs. Metters?"

"He was a sixteen-year-old boy, Mr. McGuire. How could he?"

Ted White stood and released his hand from his mother's grip. He moved toward the door with a look on his face that did not bode well for Jessie Preece.

Bud managed to get to the front porch steps as White, already in the sheriff's car, turned the ignition and began backing out of the drive. Bud moved as quickly as he could toward the cruiser. White saw him, stopped and waited.

"Deputy White," Bud said, leaning on the door of the car and breathing heavily. "Ted," he said, "by all rights other than Virginia law, this is my case. Let me be there."

"Get in," White said and revved the engine impatiently.

Ted White thumped on the door to Jessie Preece's dwelling with a heavy fist, startling Bud with the intensity of the sudden blows in the mountain's nighttime silence. Preece's house was isolated, up a steep hill and set into heavy woods off the road. The house might have once been well kept.

"Uncle Jessie," Ted called out, banging on the door again.

Bud heard movement from inside. "Open up, Jessie. It's Ted."

After a minute the door opened revealing a living room cluttered with ragged furniture and a table littered with unwashed cups and plates. A dim light bulb hanging by a cord from the ceiling revealed little else. An unpleasant odor occupied the room. Preece looked frightened.

White made Preece sit down in a dingy chair while he and Bud stood. Preece stared up at Bud and his nephew.

"Uncle Jessie, I'm here about that skeleton from the cave. You tell me now…did you kill that German prisoner?"

"No."

"You saw my mother up there with him. You saw what

they did. You told her he was never coming back. She told me that, Jessie, and don't you tell me she's a liar."

"I don't think I did," Preece said.

"Tell me what happened."

Preece admitted he followed Vicey to the overlook, where she met Weissmann. When Vicey left, Jessie remained, hidden behind the darkness of the trees, watching Weissmann and hating him for what he saw him do.

"I waited for him to pass by where I was hidden. When he did, I hit him over the head with a big rock. He fell down. I beat on him bad, Ted."

"Go on."

"I went home and waited for Adron to come in. I told him what I did. Adron wanted to see the dead body, so he drove me back up the hill to the overlook. But he wadn't dead."

"Weissman was alive?"

"He was blowin' little short breaths and stuff was runnin' out his nose and mouth."

"My God," Bud heard White mutter.

"Neither one of us wanted to touch him," Preece said, continuing. "Adron wanted me to hit him with the rock until he was dead, but I couldn't do it no more."

"Finish it," White said, coldly.

As Preece told it, the two boys rode back down the mountain and found rope and chains, and returned near daylight. They anchored the chains to a tree and the two boys lowered Weissmann over the precipice. Adron, secured to a safety line, rappelled down the face of the cliff to a cave he knew about. Weissmann was left in the cave to die.

"Did Banner know?" Bud asked.

"No. Then Adron joined the Army 'bout a month later, and got killed. Nobody else knew about it."

Bud said to White, "I don't know that there'll be prison records you can use to prove the skeleton belongs to Weissmann."

"Don't need 'em," White said, keeping his gaze on Preece. "A search of the cave turned up a ring like mom's, the silver one she showed you. It's all I need."

White pulled his Uncle Jessie out of the chair and pushed him roughly toward the door. He turned to Bud. "I'll drop you off at mom's." He said no more on the drive back to Vicey Metter's house.

Bud got out of the deputy's car. In the back seat, Jessie Preece was a gaunt and forsaken creature.

Bud looked through the open window at Ted White, who had learned perhaps too much about himself for one day.

"Deputy White," Bud said, "your Uncle Jessie is a pitiful old man who committed murder when he was a boy. He's had to live with that. You're a fine deputy. Someday you'll make a fine sheriff. You go do your duty. And no more."

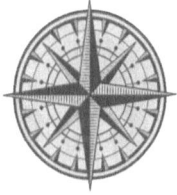

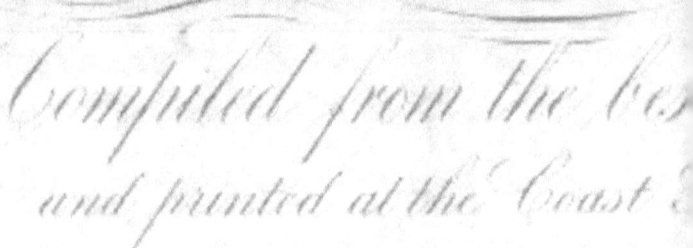

Compiled from the be...

and printed at the Coast ...

A.D. Bache, Su...

May 1864.

Scale of Miles

NOTES

Area of State .... 61,352 sq. miles
Number of Counties 163 *Richmond, Capital of State. Population in 1860, 37,910*

Population of State, Census of 1860, Whites 1,047,411
Free Colored 58,042
Slaves 490,865

Total Population of State 1,596,318

Number of Miles of Rail Roads in operation (in 1860) 1,731
Canals 230
(Not including Canals in connection with improved River Navigation)
Total Rail Roads in United States & Territories (in 1860) 30,793,597

DISTANCES by RAIL ROADS.

New York to Philadelphia	87
Philadelphia to Baltimore	98
Baltimore to Washington	40
Harrisburg to Baltimore	84
Annapolis to Washington	42
Wheeling to Washington	404
Wheeling to Baltimore	379
Wheeling to Grafton	100
Parkersburg to Grafton	104
Grafton to Cumberland	101
Cumberland to Harpers Ferry	97
Harpers Ferry to Washington	103
Harpers Ferry to Winchester	32
Alexandria to Leesburg	38
Alexandria to Manassas Junction	27
Manassas Junction to Manassas Gap	46
Manassas Gap to Strasburg	15
Strasburg to McCheck...	43
Alexandria to Richmond	
to Fredericksburg & Potomac R.R.	63
Fredericksburg to Aquia Creek (by steamer)	10
Aquia Creek to Fredericksburg	15

uthorities

y Office.

Elizabethtown

Parkersburg

Charleston

TILDEN M. "TIM" COUNTS, JR., PH.D.

Tilden M. "Tim" Counts, Jr., Ph.D. spent his childhood in Tazewell, Virginia. As a teenager, his family relocated to Wauchula, Florida. He attended Staunton Military Academy, received his undergraduate and master's degrees from the University of Kentucky, and later earned his doctorate from the University of North Carolina at Chapel Hill.

Tim's career in education included positions at Temple University, Florida Southern College, and the University of South Florida, Tampa.

Today, he lives in Mint Hill, North Carolina where he is fully enjoying his retirement with his wife, Mona, and his pitbull, Jack.

www.ingramcontent.com/pod-product-compliance
Lightning Source LLC
Chambersburg PA
CBHW050938120626
46552CB00001B/278